DITA SAXOVA

Dita Saxova

ARNOŠT LUSTIG

Translated from the Czech
by Jeanne Němcová

HARPER & ROW, PUBLISHERS

NEW YORK, HAGERSTOWN
SAN FRANCISCO, LONDON

1817

FIRST EDITION

Designed by C. Linda Dingler

Library of Congress Cataloging in Publication Data

Lustig, Arnošt.
  Dita Saxova.
  Translation of Dita Saxová.
  I. Title.
PZ4.L97Dk 1979   [PG5038.L85]   891.8'6'35   78–69505
ISBN 0–06–012712–0

79 80 81 82 83 10 9 8 7 6 5 4 3 2 1

Everything is possible if we want it.
We will join hands,
And on the ruins of the ghetto, we will laugh.
—FROM THE SONG OF AN UNKNOWN SINGER,
THERESIENSTADT
1942–1943

If a bear chases you, you will be troubled
by an enemy. If you kill the bear
or elude it, it is a sign that you will
overcome your troubles.
—BOOK OF DREAMS
1948

DITA SAXOVA

one

They'll listen and they won't understand.
—JEWISH GAZETTE

The best weapon against a submarine is still a submarine.
—JEWISH GAZETTE

1

Isabela Goldblatova's seven cats were prowling through the girls' hostel at 53 Lublania Street, and Lev Goldblat, the custodian nicknamed For-Better-For-Worse, didn't even notice. Among the messages he had found in the china cupboard was an accusation. The informant—he had no doubt it was one of the girls—stated what she had heard through the door when only Dita Saxova was home. And that these confidences had undoubtedly been intended for Dita's ears.

It was an old house, just like all the others on Lublania Street, built at the end of the nineteenth century or at the beginning of this one. It had four stories, an attic, and a big cellar; and even before the war it had belonged to the Jewish Community. During the war the Nazis had used it as a warehouse for prayer books and other entertaining literature, for musical instruments, pianos, harps, clarinets, and so on. Later the building was turned into a hostel and school for army nurses on their way to and from the Eastern Front.

Lev Goldblat was crossing the former school kitchen, which he had converted into an apartment after the war. He was surprised by all the details in the note. According to the informant, Alfred Neugeborn, nineteen, from the boys' hostel on Krakovska Street, had his eye on the safe of the Social Welfare Committee in the Jewish Religious Community building. Either tomorrow or the day after, the anonymous writer alleged, Neugeborn intended to break into the cellar from Maislova Street in the Old Town, and make his way up the stairs past the ritual kitchen and the elevator into the room opposite the registration office and archives, where the safe was.

Lev Goldblat visualized the cashier's window with the wire grill. The note, scribbled on a page torn from a school notebook, ended with the date: Friday, February 28, 1947.

"Has anyone been inquiring about Dita?"

"Some clerk from the statistics office," said Isabela.

"You didn't ask what he wanted?"

The note pointed out that if Neugeborn, otherwise known as Fitzi, who was about to finish his apprenticeship as a locksmith, took the money he would ruin his whole future. And as for Dita Saxova, she only went to that school of hers to get out of doing any proper work; in fact she was nothing but a *parasite*.

Between the soup and the fried carp—the menu on most winter Fridays—Lev Goldblat, pretending to be careful about bones, pondered over each girl.

At meetings of the cultural or study commissions (she wasn't in the religious one), Dita suggested that the Community buy an original Chagall for the big room downstairs where there were dances sometimes on Saturdays. Dita was well known for her stinging remarks. When Mr. A. F. spoke about the efforts of the Czech government in exile in London, she handed him a slip of paper with a Chinese proverb on it: "The more you speak, the less people remember." Mr. A. F. replied to her disarming smile with a French saying that a smile is no indication that the person who smiles is happy. *"Chere amie,"* he said to her, *"ce n'est pas être bien aise que de rire."* In the end he invited her to have lunch with him. She ordered roast duck.

And Alfred Neugeborn? What did he know of the boy? Lev

Goldblat thought. Mr. Traxler, the superintendent of the hostel at 24 Krakovska, allowed him to go out on all sorts of repair jobs, so he was earning more than any of the other boys. He had repaired the stair railing at 53 Lublania free of charge—though actually the house needed a new railing, an investment they couldn't put off indefinitely.

Last spring Dita had disappeared for three days. She had returned to the garrison at Theresienstadt, the former camp where she had been with her mother and father in 1942 and 1943 before they were separated in the fall of 1944 at Auschwitz-Birkenau. She brought back a pair of shoes with cardboard soles, and cherished them as a talisman still.

Besides that, it was said that she'd had an affair with a gigolo from the local Jewish bar—or, to be more exact, from a bar which, like the Ascherman Cafe in Dlouha Street, at the beginning of the war had catered exclusively to the "inferior races" and after the war continued to maintain a predominantly Jewish clientele. The gigolo was an Austrian by birth who made his living as a ski instructor. Someone said that once, when Dita had gone to the bar with Mr. A. F., the gigolo had made eyes at her and, when she went to the powder room, had stopped her and invited her to spend three days in the mountains, saying he'd teach her to ski if she didn't know how, or perfect her style if she already skied a little. If one could judge by who did the most talking, then Linda Huppertova knew the most details, but at the same time this was also a good reason for doubting the story.

It was said that the gigolo was a former Austrian champion in slalom and downhill racing, a claim which in itself gave cause for doubt. It was said that he had taken Dita to a mountain lodge, where he had wined and dined her and promised to reveal to her the difference between a boy and a man. According to Linda Huppertova, his age was somewhere between twenty-one and thirty-one. Later he had asked Dita to pay for the ski lessons, but since she had no money and refused to pay, he had taught her for free. He skied down the slopes like a dancer, and was so elegant and self-assured doing a christiania that Dita had been filled with admiration. When she had refused to go to bed with him, he had asked her at least to spend the evening with him. The gigolo drank a lot, which was supposedly the reason Dita came back a day early. At first he hadn't told her anything, but later he had admitted that he lived with older women, kept them company, and let them pay for his services.

There was too much "supposedly" and "maybe" and "probably" in it. But it occurred to the custodian that, although Dita hadn't gone with the gigolo, she might have, even though he knew the exact reason for Dita's three-day absence. She had caught a cold when visiting Theresienstadt and had almost come down with pneumonia. Most of the time she was a happy creature, but sometimes there seemed to be something in her that made her afraid. For a minute, he imagined Dita Saxova in the mountains with an unknown stranger. He could imagine her as pretty enough for the prettiness to pass for strength, and as smiling enough to suggest equanimity and maturity.

According to the unwritten rules, the custodian never asked unnecessary questions. Now he was thinking that everything had its limits.

Right after the war Dita had been hired to work in the archives. She grumbled that it was no fun messing around in dusty files. She confessed to Munk, who was in charge of the auxiliary evening school class here, that she would like to learn to draw or to do something related to the theater—some profession in which she would be free. She admitted that this also was "probably more a matter of inclination than of real talent." Dita was eighteen, but she often behaved or talked as if she were thirty.

Her roommates in room 16 were Brigita Mannerheimova and Liza Vagnerova. Brigita—also known as Holy Virgin or Brita—had acne and thick arms and legs, and she usually had to spend two or three days in bed each month as if she were sick.

Liza Vagnerova, with her wide mouth and thick bluish lips, had been having an affair with a doctor from the local clinic.

In number 15, the room next door, lived Linda Huppertova,

the stepsister of D. E. Huppert. She was working as an apprentice in Madame Schiller's dressmaking salon on the corner of Lublania and Legerova streets. Some time ago, as everyone knew by now, she had taken a box of clothing that belonged to Alexander Lebovitch, a friend of Neugeborn's who had stayed with her overnight, and sold it the next day to a secondhand dealer.

Tonitchka Blauova, the smallest girl in the hostel, also lived in number 15. She had been raped during the war. Sometimes she would cry out at night—words or sentences that nobody could understand.

After supper Lev Goldblat played his battered Italian mandolin. Isabela washed the dishes. She eyed her cutlery, which had been hidden for her throughout the war and restored to her afterward. She didn't ask him questions anymore. Looking a little guilty, she glanced at an old photograph behind the frosted glass of the china cupboard. It showed their three sons, none of whom had come back after the war. They occupied her thoughts by day and her dreams by night.

If you were lucky, she thought, you might get your cutlery back from the people who took it when the war started, but that was about all. Even the Friday fish was no longer the ceremonial affair it used to be. But then, what was? There had been changes in their food too.

Lev Goldblat hung his mandolin over the trunk where the feather quilts were stored. He imagined himself back in Trieste during the First World War, when he used to get up to reveille and go to bed with the sob of taps.

His head was filled with thoughts of the denunciation. What if the allegation was false? His dinner was definitely spoiled. Finally he thought about Alfred Neugeborn and what he had to do with Dita Saxova.

2

The day before that Friday night had threatened snow and frost since morning. Dita Saxova had been keeping an eye on the pinkish-brown tint of clouds and smoke hanging low over the rooftops.

She had to go downstairs to pick up her phonograph because yesterday evening some younger girls on the second floor had wanted to play some records. She carried it upstairs as though it were a piece of luggage and she were setting out on a journey. She lay down on her stomach, her chin propped on her hands, staring at the floor. She liked to stretch out like this, before her bath, on the Chinese mat they used as a carpet.

She began to leaf through a magazine of Brita's to pass the time. Beautifully dressed women smiled at her from the glossy pages, and companies with fancy-sounding foreign names displayed full-page advertisements for cigarettes and wristwatches. Quite a different world from that of the *Jewish Gazette,* a copy of which Liza had left lying on her bed. It was easy to notice the contrast. It would all fit onto the head of a pin, she decided.

She had always liked advertisements, though she couldn't have said why; perhaps because, like her phonograph, they represented entertainment and a good life, and she could imagine herself with all the lavish goods offered there. These particular advertisements in Brita's glossy magazine, decorated with coats of arms reminiscent of royalty, came, she noticed now, from Switzerland.

She sighed involuntarily and turned back to the *Gazette.* It was pure chance that she should find in it a speech made by the Community warehouseman, ex-Sergeant-Major Julius Schwartz. Viewed in retrospect, it was in the nature of a last will and testament. He had jumped out of a window because someone had accused him of joining the army only at the eleventh hour. She found herself feeling annoyed with this man. He had spoiled her pleasure in those noble Swiss advertisements. Nothing like what they offered was to be found here. She tried to read on, but foundered in a long article by someone who performed an acrobatic dance among the paragraphs of the Civil Code, to determine whether or not some old man in Varnsdorf who had spent the war years in England should be entitled to get his factory back when other factories of the same kind were being nationalized. Her anger against the dead warehouseman increased. She couldn't explain it, but there it was, tangible and insistent.

She picked up Brita's lavish magazine again, but the joy was gone. It was just a curious trick of fate that had caused her to be born at 7 Josefovska Street instead of as the daughter of some Aryan aristocrat, as Dr. Fitz had said. This foreign way of life, lived by aliens in alien countries, gave her a strange feeling.

Once, she remembered, her father had told her about an American actress, Marion Davies, who had fifty bathrooms in her house, each one of them a different color. What Pied Piper of Hamelin had lured this little Marion in that direction as a child? Erich Munk would know the answers, of course. Nevertheless, castes and classes *did* exist, and they were to blame for the curse of loneliness. Dita knew that too, even if she refused to acknowledge it.

She thought about how they felt here about each other. About Tonitchka, how nice she looked from time to time, and what she might have been if the war hadn't come. Perhaps that was the reason she had her photograph taken so often, and looked at the pictures when she was alone, as if she didn't really believe she was so pretty.

She thought about how she'd taken care of children in Theresienstadt. She used to put them to bed and tell them about how the world was going to be someday. She thought about the men who used to hang around her then, and she'd never known why. Later, at the Buna Werke in Auschwitz-Birkenau bei Neuberun, she carried rocks with a man who always took the heavier ones so she wouldn't have to.

Then she thought about how Linda Huppertova gossiped about, among other things, the last year in the life of the alleged gigolo. The gigolo, according to Linda, had recently lived with one older woman for three years. She had taken him to Italy on the *Leonardo da Vinci*. One day during the trip he had told her that he'd like to end the affair, and she had seemed to take it in her stride. In the evening they had gone to bed as usual. In the morning, Dita's gigolo woke up, but his companion slept on and on. He called the doctor, and there had been a scandal which had even involved the captain. Apparently she had left an empty bottle of sleeping pills and a farewell note for him, but the captain had impounded it, so he never even knew what she'd said. It was lucky the old lady hadn't died, but they had almost locked him up, and the rest of the cruise had been hopeless. Everyone had pointed a finger at him: "There goes the gigolo. Look, that's the gigolo." But the captain hadn't given the letter to the police, so everything had turned out okay.

Dita thought about other girls, their mothers, where they had died, whether they wanted children or not and why, and what they expected. And she thought again about her mind and her body, and whether to use it for security or not. If I cannot, then am I really left on my own? How can I rely on myself and not on men? How much do I need of feelings and luck? There was also a question of how many of her own feelings she was entitled to, how many unconditional approvals she should yield to. My God, she thought to herself, I hope I won't be like those people who have a moral crisis every seven seconds.

She had her own secret theory about happiness. She imagined it as an invisible constellation of stars you couldn't touch, in which each star rotates for everybody's personal happiness in strange, undetermined circles. You may catch one because by some chance it's in the same orbit, but you can't hold on to it very long because everything is in constant motion. Or else you miss it. But then you wait until another one comes along. It depends on how long you live.

She stretched out her long legs and stuck her feet into a new pair of red slippers, which she had bought, after some deliberation, to replace her old ones. She was proud of the phonograph; it came from England, and it seemed that everything "made in England" was really good. She had got it from the Aid for Repatriates sale last summer. She just walked into the shop and bought it on the spur of the moment, without first asking its price. She had had to combat the same habit of thriftiness from which Tonitchka and Linda suffered notoriously, the impulse to save everything prudently as a nest egg, or at least to spend it on food, as the others did. She entertained no futile illusions about the future, but at the same time she waited to see what it would bring. She both wanted and did not want to have everything that the savings books promised, yet she felt a strong revulsion against acting as if some catastrophe were going to strike again tomorrow. In this respect she thought of herself as being somewhat superior to the others.

Room 16 was a haven for Isabela Goldblatova's cats. Dita was one of the few girls who actually knew the names of those seven feline beauties, knew what each one of them liked best to eat, and knew how to fondle them. She would stroke with the whole palm of the hand, gently and lazily, knead the fur between slightly spread fingers, or scratch the cat's throat and belly while she talked. Liza Vagnerova, on the other hand, didn't like cats; they pulled threads out of the mat and played with them, and she complained that one of these days the girls would find their lingerie full of fleas. But apart from one isolated case that had turned the whole house upside down, nothing of the sort had happened. As for Brita Mannerheimova, where cats were concerned she couldn't have cared less.

3

Dita put in a new phonograph needle, a gift from Neugeborn. He could get almost any metal item from the locksmith's shop where he worked.

She listened to the record and to the noises in number 15, next door. It sounded like Linda Huppertova rummaging in little Tonitchka's things. Everybody still seemed to think that Tonitchka had a treasure hidden in her mattress.

Dita began to brush her hair, one hundred and fifty strokes on each side. She was wondering what to wear to the party tomorrow evening. Last time she had worn her skirt with a half slip with lace edging, a belt, a navy blue crepe de chine blouse with a bow and a sleeveless red vest. She had sacrificed three-quarters of her monthly stipend for that outfit.

The black cat, Crista, was staring down at her from the top of the wardrobe. Polish could not hide the scratches that showed through. Is it true that cats—faithful only to their surroundings, not to man—cannot be trained like dogs, lions, or apes in the circus? The cat spat and mewed; devotion, genuine or false, shone in her bright green eyes. Some spilled washing powder, which no one had yet thought of brushing up and putting back into its box, showed white beneath the crate. Dita watched the cat and brushed her hair.

Fleetingly she felt a pang of conscience for the morning of class she had missed at the School of Applied Arts. The afternoon sky was still bright. The snow outside was very white. Probably because of that word "class," which may have hidden implications, I can plunge into a lot of things with a verve that deserves a better cause, and then deceive myself, she thought. If she went outside now, the man who ran the bar across the street would probably invite her in for a glass of tea with rum, to show her that he thought her sufficiently grown up.

Dita wound up the phonograph. Sometimes these same melodies meant different things for her. It was as if she were looking into a mirror, and besides what was there now she could see what had been there before and sometimes what would be in the future.

Pleased with her hair, she glimpsed the cat's green eyes behind her. Fortunately Munk had enough tact not to remind her about the books. Thanks to them, she had managed to accumulate a bit more spending money from time to time. Most of the time she bought flowers. "If a couple of chocolate bars went along with it, somebody might get suspicious about you and Fatty," Liza had told her. "When it's only books, it's still platonic. Even with dinner invitations, it's still a chaste love."

Munk, whenever he came to room 16, would stand outside

and knock repeatedly, as though he suspected they were all running around in their undies. Once he was inside, he would listen to her with an impatient smile on his lips, and recommend good reading matter. Was he pleasantly surprised and relieved, or disappointed, to find that they were not in the habit of wandering around half naked? He too was fond of *The Threepenny Opera,* and even knew the German lyrics by heart. But he didn't dare sing.

"Quiet!" Linda Huppertova screeched from next door. Dita waited for a moment and then turned down the phonograph.

4

Half an hour later a small man dressed in a gray business suit stood in the doorway. There was still snow on his overcoat. He explained to her that he had come about a matter concerning her uncle.

Dita asked him which uncle he had in mind and invited him into the room.

"It's a nice place you've got here," he said, looking around him. "An interesting house."

"A better kind of orphanage," Dita answered.

"Uncle Carl," the man told her.

She flushed. In Birkenau, Uncle Carl had worked in the Jewish *Sonderkommando* as a dentist.

"Won't you sit down?"

"I've waited all this time in case any of your family tried to contact me. Finally I found your address here. I'm entering the civil service. We were friends of your uncle even in the toughest times. It's really nicer here than I expected."

Cautiously the man took a seat. "There were extremely stiff penalties for looking after the former Jewish property. May I ask you a few questions, just for the record?"

When he sat down, the difference in their heights disappeared. He asked her when she had seen her uncle for the last time.

"He wrote to us from Heydebreck in September 1943. It was

a code word. The date was wrong too. When Mother got his postcard in Theresienstadt they had all gone up the chimney already."

"You mean to say they weren't there anymore?"

"I'm afraid so."

"They killed them? I see," said the man.

"I can turn the light on," suggested Dita.

"Were you all at the same address?"

"In the fall of 1943 most people went to the Family Camp in Birkenau."

"What were they told?"

"That they were going to settle in empty land. On the ramp they told them to hurry up and take a bath before the trip."

"The Family Camp, you said? Did your uncle work all that time at his own profession?"

He studied her oval face—the skin with the color of an unripe peach, the sharply etched blue eyes, and the forehead with its fine furrows. When she smiled, she revealed two rows of white teeth. One tooth was the color of ivory and protruded a bit. She ran her fingers through her hair.

"I was under the impression that you had already consulted your lawyer," the man said. He was again looking around him and saw the phonograph, the red carnation in the milk bottle, and the map from Mobil Oil on the wall.

"A lot of places have opened up now for folks like you. Everywhere you look, people have had to leave their jobs. Now's your chance. You haven't been mixed up in anything. And you don't need to feel like you're under a magnifying glass."

She laughed.

She remembered that old Grandmother Olga on her mother's side used to own a small plot of land in the village of Habry near Golcuv Jenikov. She had never gone back to claim it, of course. It hadn't seemed worth trying to tie herself down to that little piece of land just to lose it again. And why should one turn to past destiny and destroy future fate? she thought.

The man looked at her. "The danger's over. Now's your

chance," he repeated. "They're still firing people who bet on the wrong horse during the war. This is your opportunity."

Until just before the war, Dita's parents had owned a laundry on Josefovska Street. Her father had sold it in the summer of 1939, just in time. She wondered whether he hadn't sold it only for appearance' sake, the way people get married or divorced these days.

"At least we learned how to survive," the man said. "They've put you back together again quickly though. Do they pay for your electricity too?" He fingered the lock on his briefcase. "We all lived through it. We lived through all kinds of things, didn't we? It's all just a matter of survival."

She heard him and wore her vague little smile, as if she were smiling to herself. Once she'd asked her father why Uncle Carl was usually so sad. "Don't you know why?" Daddy asked her. "Don't you know nobody likes dentists, that most folks are scared of them?" So why didn't he become a chimney sweep, she had wondered?

Dita remembered her father. During the war he had looked like a cartoon from *Stürmer:* small, shabby, and threadbare. Mother was a pretty blonde with a nice figure. Maybe she had married beneath her station. Perhaps Dita had inherited her anxiety, veiled in their yearning to live in a nice white house someday. But if in those days Daddy hadn't believed even a bit that they would get out of it alive, he probably would not have learned to be a cobbler at his age.

"Is it true what they say, that your people are eternal?" the man asked. There was almost an echo of reproach in his voice.

Dita kept her silent smile and didn't answer. Just as Andy and Fitzi and D. E. had learned during the war, she'd found out how to judge people's character quickly—by their faces, their eyes, scars, wrinkles, and by their voices; to determine from a few sentences, what was important for them and what wasn't, putting together in a few seconds their whole lives, what was behind them and what was ahead, so she would know what kind of people they were, what she could expect from them and what she couldn't. She needed very little to compose a portrait of a person and she remembered it for a long time.

"They put all of you together this way." the man repeated. "That's really not such a bad idea. . . . It's a good idea. Everything's easier when you're together. At your age . . . that's the way times are now. . . . This is really a very interesting place."

The man took a small packet out of his briefcase. "These are sheets of gold foil, Miss Saxova. Here's your half of what he left with me. You use it as you think best. It's twenty-two-carat gold. Just to give you an idea, rings are made from ten-carat today." He laid the little package on Brita's bed.

Her throat tightened and she tried to save the situation by saying, "Excuse me." She remembered the classified ad she'd cut out of an old newspaper that morning for Tonitchka: "Aches and pains? Use Feller's Fluid, with the label 'Elsafluid.' Try our rhubarb pills."

"What did you do there? Is it true that everybody, without exception, had to work as long as they were still alive?"

"I looked after children for a while."

"Do you like children?"

"That was a long time ago."

"Did any of them come back?"

"Possibly."

The man looked down at the little parcel of gold foil.

She lowered her chin and watched him attentively.

"Everything is relative," the visitor said, smiling. "There is no absolute moral code. Ninety-nine percent of everything that's important in life revolves around money," he added.

"Thank you," said Dita. She began to blush again. Her heart pounded.

"I thank you too," said the man casually. "It was my duty. I cared for it as if it were my own. It was my method of resistance. The Gestapo had more than five thousand men in Bohemia. A rope or a bullet solved everything. I was waiting for you to get in touch with me yourself. I hope this has not been a surprise for you."

"Not too much," she lied. She was used to having people

think her smile was a sign of self-confidence.

"You can deposit this in any bank."

"Is there any way I can thank you for it?"

For a moment he looked at her.

"A cup of tea?" she offered.

"No, thank you. Now I must really be going."

"No receipt?"

"Can't we consider the matter closed by shaking hands?"

"It's still snowing," Dita said.

"Fortunately, I don't have very far to go," the man answered.

5

For the next half hour Dita stared at the little package. At first she thought that the man had not understood when she acted as if the tooth gold were distasteful to her, despite her gratitude for his having given it to her.

She inhaled deeply. So all this was life. Uncle Carl. Ladies and gentlemen, you have to take a shower. The tooth gold. ("Gold is so good that in the last six, or even in the last six thousand, years they've never found anything better or tougher," the man had said, and smiled. "Who knows what will happen after all the gold in the world is gone?") It was property. And she had gotten it easily, the way everything had come to her so far. She turned on the phonograph again.

He had gone to a lot of trouble wrapping the package. What to do with all this twine? She had reached Auschwitz-Birkenau in the autumn of 1944. She stood with Mother in front of the soldier who was supervising the distribution of underwear. He wore black riding boots and a clean shirt with his frog-green uniform. With a jerk of his thumb he signaled Mother to move aside. Dita knelt in front of him and pleaded for her mother. His eyes, as he looked down at her, were empty, yet they had all the power in the world.

He kicked her. She was almost glad when she fell, face in the mud.

When the girls had had a few friends in last Friday evening, they talked about Switzerland. D. E. Huppert said he suspected that Swiss banks had safes stuffed with tooth gold, the property of German officers who had deposited it in numbered accounts.

D. E. told her not to let that change her mind, or what crazy Munk said, either. ("Switzerland must be a beautiful country!")

Snow was tumbling fast on the other side of the window. The sky hung low. The song on the phonograph droned on about how, last night under a yellow moon, a girl had rejected her lover.

6

"Of course, they could have bought a better house," suggested Dita. She knew how much pleasure it gave Linda to eavesdrop. It was as if she could look through the walls too. She looked at her. "You've got blood on your lip. Don't you want to wipe it off before it trickles down your chin?"

Linda pulled out a handkerchief. She wiped the blood off her lip and chin. Dita got down from the windowsill. She turned down the phonograph.

"If you tell Dr. Fitz you've got periodontitis and your teeth are crumbling, you might as well enclose an 'official request.' "

One of the shoes with cardboard soles lay on the bed next to the little packet of gold foil. Linda picked up its mate. "You want to wear this cardboard junk to the party tomorrow?"

"What do you think I ought to wear?"

Linda was in no hurry to answer. She wondered why Dita hadn't even asked the man his name and address.

Dita put on the shoe and laced it up. Linda didn't dare touch the package. She had not gone to work for the same reason as Dita.

Last Friday Dita had had company: students and friends, including Linda's stepbrother, D. E. Huppert. They sang, yelled, and laughed. They ate potato pancakes with garlic, which Dita made with Isabela Goldblatova's help, and served with tea. And they listened to "Ti-pi-tin," and sang, "One night when the moon was so mellow . . ."

When the potato pancakes ran out, Lebovitch began to grumble that the Promised Land (capital P, capital L) was so far away, as if someone were to blame. To change the subject, Fischer (a junior at Charles University Law School) began to praise the Danish monarchy.

It didn't even occur to D. E. to knock at the door to number 15. Dita quoted him some lines about her heroine, Agnes, from Viktor Dyk's 1911 version of the *Pied Piper of Hamelin,* with his Mr. R. C., or Rat Catcher: "A person should not consume himself the measure of love that is meant for two."

She pressed on with more quotations: "There is only a certain degree of love, and it is limited and unchangeable. Do not love too much, if you want to be loved. . . . An overflowing measure of the love you give destroys the chances for the love you should receive." Mr. R. C. was the Pied Piper himself. She didn't feel the slightest compunction at misquoting him. (She knew the book almost by heart, and was very proud of the fact; she had found in it some bitter mystery, and an unfathomable beauty of word and meaning.)

"Ti-pi-tin" was an anthem for them. Dita's laughter drowned out everything unpleasant that might recall them to the hostel at 53 Lublania and its cautious custodian. When she laughed, people thought she was grown up.

As long as Linda Huppertova had been living in number 15—twenty-one months—all sorts of things had gone on next door on Friday evenings. Sometimes it ended with dancing, sometimes in silence. For Linda the silence was always the puzzle.

"Don't you agree that every girl ought to have an unexpected inheritance, sort of a miracle in our time, every now and then?" Dita asked. "Or at least that some well-heeled organization should give her an extra welfare check?"

"Are you going tomorrow?"

Linda was thinking that if she had been in Dita's place, she would have squeezed more out of that fellow who had looked after the gold for her. She tossed the other shoe back on the bed. The little packet bounced.

"On account of my crazy shoes, you mean?"

Linda had bulging green eyes and a neck like a turtle's from which protruded her head with its shock of brown hair. She glanced at Liza's bed.

"Some people's souls have been crippled past recognition," Dita observed. She didn't explain herself and Linda didn't ask. Whenever Dita tried to understand Linda's impulses—now, yesterday—the one that suggested itself was fear. Of all the girls, Linda was the most afraid. She had enough fear inside her for the next ninety years.

"Herbert Lagus still likes you?" she asked.

"I don't know," said Dita. "Maybe, maybe not."

"How much do you care for him?"

"Not the way he needs."

"At least somebody likes you," Linda said abruptly.

Linda peered into the open chest of drawers where Dita kept her underwear. White, beige, and blue. She dreamed of champagne satin. But such underwear didn't exist in Prague.

"I bet that as a child you wore a broad-brimmed hat, like a boarding-school girl," Linda said. "Dresses with lace collars and patent leather shoes. What plans do you have for yourself?"

"I've still got some time before I go out on the streets."

"Girls like you don't do that." Linda knew that Dita hardly ever talked about her plans, which made her all the more interesting.

"Who knows what I'm going to have to do finally, once I discover I don't have a single duke in my family tree," said Dita. "Or that among those I do manage to find, no one's a banker."

Linda raised her eyebrows.

"You know the song that goes like this?" Dita went back to the phonograph and turned the record over. *"Now I go to sleep. When I wake up in the morning, life will be changed for the better."*

"Is that on the other side?"

"No, it's another song. *You believe that? I don't. Maybe.*"

Offended, Linda drew in her neck. Dita tied the sash of her kimono with its Japanese designs. Linda's face was wooden. The record came to an end and Dita began to hum, "Gentlemen come to us every day!"

Linda turned in the doorway. For some seconds she fought the impulse to shriek out that Dita was nothing but a bitch. Her lips were twisted awry, as if she had drunk wormwood.

"They come here often enough, don't they?" she asked.

7

Linda Huppertova, who whispered boastfully at house meetings that she had finished her apprenticeship and would be able to earn her own living any day now, had the reputation in the hostel of a busybody. Given the opportunity, she would pry into anything and everything that didn't concern her and was none of her business. Tonitchka Blauova was her most frequent victim.

Rarely did Linda miss a tidbit of gossip about someone else, such as the affairs of Doris Lewittova, who had been practically expelled from the hostel after her pregnancy was discovered (though a nice place for her to stay had been arranged), and she had tried diligently to alter her condition by allowing as many boys as possible into her bed. It seemed that Linda was the only one who knew about Doris's two maiden aunts, and about the connection between their spinsterhood and their niece's behavior. Linda knew down to the last detail who had been bawled out by the superintendent, and who had had an affair with whom, beginning with Liza Vagnerova, in whose bed Isabela Goldblatova had once discovered the district physician. After that the offender had been replaced by Dr. Fitz, while Liza had taken up with Mr. Maximilian Gotlob, who was twice her age but had a good position in the International Blue and White Student Union. Linda knew how many years old Munk still had to work before he could claim a full pension, and how long it was since Dita Saxova had done any real work.

Linda Huppertova had a nose like a bloodhound. That same Friday afternoon, as she was keeping her customary watch on the whole corridor, she saw through the ever-open crack of her door the arrival of Alfred Neugeborn.

Fitzi's sallow hand smoothed the rickety banisters he had recently repaired. Just before he reached the door of room 16 he took a nosegay of snowdrops from its tissue paper wrapper. (Linda assessed their value as at least five crowns.) He passed by her door, quite unaware of the disappointment he was causing her, for he was as innocent of her presence as he was of her greedy wish that he would transfer his attentions to another room and another of the hostel's residents.

She heaved an involuntary sigh, the high color in her cheeks fading. The gusty sound had been quite loud, and she wouldn't have minded at all if it had reached Alfred Neugeborn's ears. She had only a nodding acquaintance with him, having met him casually both here and at the Krakovska Street socials; but if he had come to visit her, he would not have had to beg for anything that would have given him real pleasure. The real regrets in Linda's life were that she didn't have Doris Lewittova's handsome legs, that her figure didn't measure up to Brita Mannerheimova's, and she didn't have the attractive smile of Dita Saxova.

Fitzi was knocking now on Dita's door and waiting to be admitted. As it had once before that same afternoon, the response came in a singsong: "Come in!" Linda Huppertova, listening, interpreted the tone as expressing Dita's world-weariness and lack of enthusiasm for the visits her neighbor would gladly have received herself. Surreptitiously she peered out through the crack of her door at Fitzi, and even whispered his name, at once admiring and condemning his lankiness.

"You're home all alone?" he said by way of greeting.

"For a while," Dita said.

He shut the door behind him. He had come in a nicely ironed blue shirt with white stripes and a wine-colored ascot tie. His carefully combed hair was wavy, bleached at the ends by the summer sun, and parted on the left. His nose was flattened and his jaw had been broken since he had learned to box with Andy Lebovitch at the gym in the doctor's house. But Liza claimed that his nose had been broken long before he started boxing.

"Peace to your house. It looks here like it did in Theresienstadt during *Lichtsperre*. 'Electricity forbidden. Only candles.' " He smiled. "How are you?"

"Yesterday at little Munk's recommendation, I went to the lecture on the nationalization of factories. I took a tip from Dr. Fitz, and for two weeks I typed envelopes for the Emigration Bureau—twelve words an hour."

There was snow on the windowsill. The cats prowled silently through the room, their eyes like big wheels spinning around. Dita rubbed black Crista's fur between her fingers as if she were passing on some of her own suspect gentleness.

"I've got two movie tickets," Fitzi said.

"What if my eyes ache or I have another problem?"

Neugeborn took Munk's books off the shelf one after another. Hermann Hesse, Tolstoy, Turgenev.

"If your eyes ache, it's probably from all these books," said Fitzi. "What are they about?"

"All sorts of things. Something like a private Emigration Bureau."

Fitzi looked under the bed at a few embarrassing items of Brita's intimate attire. The presence of Brita's underwear and Dita's pretty face aroused conflicting feelings.

"The first book is about a vagabond who turns up his nose at everything that has already been experienced," Dita explained. "Other people pity and envy him; you know how it is. He is free, but he hasn't got a thing to his name."

"At least it is easy for him to move around."

"The second one is about a horse who was once young and beautiful. . . . Listen, Fitzi, do you think you could get us a stronger light bulb? And a pair of earmuffs for me?"

"Would you wear them? Does Munk know everything about horses too?"

"I don't know. The story is about an old nag who moved like a dancer when he was young, but finally no one recognized what a beauty he had been. They got rid of him because he was worn out."

"What is the third story about?"

"How people die in a civilized country. A man way on in years dreams about a beautiful woman in a sheer nightgown. She takes him to places he'd almost forgotten about because he had always expected more. That's my third story, where the Grim Reaper appears as a naked woman and offers something besides what he's normally got in stock."

"You and I have both had a glimpse of the other world," Fitzi said. "We know which one is better."

"As the French say, Fitzi, 'Dying only means going away for a long time.'" Dita smiled. "Munk keeps supplying me with fresh fodder. Would you like to read any?"

"I would rather you told me the stories." Neugeborn shifted his weight from one foot to the other. He unbuttoned his jacket. He took the movie tickets out of his pocket and began tearing them in little pieces.

"Was it a Russian movie, Fitzi? War? Corpses? Revolution?"

"An American comedy. Technicolor."

"Six of one, half a dozen of the other." She tossed her hair back. "What's the difference?"

Fitzi grimaced. He sat down on Dita's bed and leaned back against the map from Mobil Oil. He didn't even notice the packet.

"What kind of shoes do you have on?"

"You're not the first person to ask me that today. Don't you know that life isn't what we want, but what we have?"

Black Crista stared up at Fitzi with her big green eyes. She dug her claws into the cuffs of his trousers. Neugeborn kicked her away.

Dita sat down beside him. "Do you think it is an advantage, Fitzi, that all of a sudden there are so few of us? Don't you think it ought to be an advantage, if it cost such a lot?" She was thinking about how there were different rules for men and women.

Neugeborn inhaled. Her hair had a smell which reminded him of his mother's cookies. He almost heard the little sighs of her body and tried to understand them.

"Are you always in such a hurry with girls, Fitzi?"

Dita thought he looked nice, as if he had stepped out of a window display.

"Donated by the postwar Mrs. Lagusova," he explained, reading her mind.

She fastened the top button of her kimono, which made Neugeborn's thoughts go in just the opposite direction. She pulled the sash tighter. It must have been loose before too.

"Who is she? Redheaded, like Lagus? Somebody from the family?"

"She was a social worker in the Jewish Community before the war. When I was a kid, I used to get secondhand clothes from her at the end of every season."

"Won't you stay for supper, Fitzi? The girls will be back any minute. I almost thought the prewar Mrs. Lagusova had survived."

"For just a minute." He picked up a copy of the *Jewish Gazette* from Liza's bedside table.

"Liza's latest lover, Mr. Maximilian Gotlob, gave her a subscription. Nobody has raped her for a long time," said Dita.

Neugeborn turned to the back page: *Legal advice. Unregistered tax-free inheritances. Lowered tax exemptions.*

"Further down where there is a notice about bedbugs, Fitzi."

There it was: *Bedbugs and insects with larvae exterminated with cyanic acid (Cyklon B)—guaranteed results. DEPURA, officially licensed disinfection station, Prague XII, 16 Balbinova.*

Next to it was another classified ad: *Learn a trade—the cornerstone of life. For more information, write to ORT, Prague I, 6 Hastalska.*

Fitzi ripped it out, spat on it, and stuck it up next to the Dostoevsky quotation. Then he wanted to put up the other one too: *In Prague, Lodz, and now back to Prague, your friendly optician, Jan Heim. Health insurance honored.*

"You can spit on it, but don't stick that up there," said Dita.

"Her name was Hermina Lagusova," Fitzi said hoarsely. "They were looking for undernourished children. They wanted to send three of them to the mountains. I sucked my cheeks in like a chipmunk so they would take me."

"Did you get in?"

Suddenly Neugeborn's adam's apple started bobbing up and down again. As it dropped, it collided with his collar, so he opened the top button and loosened his tie.

"Nice of them to put 'Cyklon B' in parentheses," Dita remarked. "In Germany, they call it 'Uragan' now. We stick to the good old terms. 'Forgive but don't forget,' as the French say. 'Man—that word has a noble ring.' "

Fitzi finally managed to put his hand on Dita's knee.

"I'm not anybody's good-time girl, Fitzi, that's all." Gently, she removed his hand. "Ti-pi-tin" filled the room with its scratchy melody.

"Now you're going to tell me how you love me, Fitzi, right?"

"I wanted to ask you about something."

"Have I already read it?"

"I meant something that takes longer than just one evening." Fitzi's lips were pressed into a tight line.

"Isn't it funny, Fitzi?" She picked up the little parcel and put it away among her things. "The longer I live, the more people act as if I were the Salvation Army. If you hadn't torn up those movie tickets, we wouldn't have missed more than the newsreel."

Neugeborn said nothing.

"Not even a soft-boiled egg, Fitzi?"

"I'm not hungry."

"I've already seen it happen. The young lady on the park bridge," she said. "She resists the advances of the man who wants to kiss her, telling him she wants only a lasting relationship."

Fitzi stretched. He no longer had the courage to talk about his theory of the fountain pen: Whether you write with it or not, it dries up anyway.

"Maybe I need something like the Salvation Army myself, Fitzi." She smiled. "If it had been up to the Palestine or the Emigration Office, they would have put us on one of those ships like the *Exodus II* and sent us off to the Promised Land. Last week, on that very bed you're sitting on, Herbert Lagus tried to lure me into going off to San Salvador with him. His uncle Solly went ahead to try and find a house. Who doesn't hear a piper playing without hurrying after, toward his own Land of the Seven Mountains?"

"Are you going to go?"

"To produce a couple of baby Jewish Indians as my contribution to mankind?"

The phonograph record played and the needle caught among the cracks in the words about a stolen kiss. "Anyway, I'd just be there like a decoration." She put on the tea kettle.

"Maybe Herbert will come by after a while to tell us how far along they are," she said. "They are going to have a big house in Salvador with a private zoo and a two-story tower like Mr. Hemingway has near Havana."

"Did you ever hear what I did during the war?" Neugeborn looked at her face, hands, and her long fingers.

"Would you be very offended, Fitzi, if I had *not* heard about what you did? Or would you just be surprised?"

"It would be as if I said, 'Open, sesame,' in front of every lock and it opened."

"On Monday you told me you were going to buy a puppy and call him Hitler."

"The International Red Cross or some other agency in Switzerland sent some money to the welfare department. I wouldn't take it all."

"You do not want my love, only my applause." Dita took a bite of bread and butter.

"Want some money?" Fitzi reached into his pants pocket.

"Nothing ever seems to be enough for us."

"Are you not able to make a decision—and make it fast?"

"Does it include the ability to say no?"

"If you get a reputation for being indecisive, soft, and slow, a lot of people won't respect you."

She was tall and lovely, and at that moment she didn't look so proud. "You think I'm a whore, right?"

"How did you get such an idea?"

"Because you think that about all of us, don't you?' No past, no future, I don't owe anyone a thing."

"Do you really mean that?"

"No, I'm only teasing you." She smiled silently.

"Why are you so quiet?"

"I don't have anything to say."

"Aren't you scared?" asked Fitzi.

"I can only be scared of myself. And if I am not scared of myself, why should I be scared of you?"

"My own mother couldn't talk me out of it, Dita."

"How could she, Fitzi?" Dita displayed her white teeth. "You already told me. A man is two things: his word, and what he becomes in the eyes of a woman he is interested in, right? It is a pity that you are not a sailor and I am only a saint."

Neugeborn handed her a crumpled copy of the letter about the money that had been sent from Switzerland.

"It's really funny," she said. "Even if there were several crates of books like these, people like us would still insist there's a deluge coming."

He didn't answer.

"It doesn't say right here that you won't regret it, Fitzi."

"Are you coming to the party tomorrow evening?"

"I'm certainly not trying to talk you out of it, Fitzi," she said finally. "But it really would be burglary. And I'm not even sure if I am a good enough friend to bring you tripe soup in jail. You had better buy that dog, Fitzi. I would rather see *The King Doesn't Like Beef* in the theater with you tomorrow or on Sunday."

8

Lev Goldblat missed Alfred Neugeborn that night between Friday and Saturday by just a few seconds. He had told Isabela that he was going to put out rat poison. She leaned on her other arm to ease the pain in her chest.

When he reached the Jewish Religious Community building, Lev Goldblat looked around him like someone whose fate has always been to waste time. His chest was shaped like a caved-in washbasin. It didn't matter as long as he was chasing mice in his steel-rimmed spectacles, showing the smallest girls his catch so they would be scared and toughened at the same time. He didn't feel as easy about being a man hunter.

He circled the Old-New Synagogue in Maislova Street. It floated up out of the snowy street like a listing ship. He knew from experience—and not just at 53 Lublania—that when rats had had plenty to eat they would stare absently out of their holes rather than eat more than their stomachs could hold. Then he thought about how rats when they are hungry eat each other. After that he thought about the difference between hunger and insatiability.

It was an hour later when Alfred Neugeborn entered the office on the first floor of the building, drew the blackout curtains, opened the safe, examined the loot, and then after a few seconds tossed the little bundle of notes back. It had to be here, he answered his own question. Because there was a sum of money freshly arrived, and not all of it would reach those for whom it was intended in any case. What did she mean by all that talk of hers about a deluge?

In his mind, he could see Dita Saxova in Theresienstadt. She was fifteen years old and taking care of the little children. She was wearing blue shorts and a white T-shirt with a six-pointed star on it. She was tall and skinny but had already begun to bud breasts.

Back in those days he'd been one of the leaders of the Knights of the Empty Pockets. His friends always greeted him with the question "What did you steal today for supper?" They took their pick of fresh meat loaves from the German bakery while the guard dozed.

Fitzi Neugeborn stood there in front of the open safe with his knees and his buttocks pressed tight. His will and his dream were different, and so was his conscience. He ran his finger across the wrinkle in his forehead as if it were a bridge he had already crossed. "Ti-pi-tin" still rang in his ears. It had a kind of gloss, the patina of a world of boys and girls, a pond where Dita Saxova swam, the little fish everyone wished he could catch.

The English words of the song, learned by heart without any real understanding of their meaning, came to his tongue now like a sort of prayer for entrance among those to whom it belonged and who could sing it with sophistication and aplomb. There was a sadness in him; he didn't know exactly what about. And yet the song could be made to mean something new, something more, by exchanging the names of the two lovers for other names that would ring familiarly in his ears.

A little while before he had risen to his feet and stopped, picturing himself tossing bundles of bank notes at her, saying, "Here, take it! It's for you. Forget about Munk's and Dr. Fitz's revolution or don't. Care about D. E. Huppert or Herbert Lagus or don't care! And go and buy whatever you want!" It was different from the books Herbert Lagus carried around when he wanted to show off. Different from the house awaiting the next emigrant in San Salvador. Or different from when Dita had taken his concert tickets when he had been unable to go with her. She invited Huppert and sat beside him, well dressed and listening to *Eine Kleine Nachtmusik,* beaming like Thomas Alva Edison's wife after he had invented the lightbulb.

He'd never found the key to her that would have opened her up the way you open the lock of a door into a room, so he could see what was really inside.

Time heals all wounds; it would be most unfair if it healed them only for other people. Surely it could easily absorb a small villainy like this in a matter of months, even weeks. He could not get rid of the feeling that he was the victim of some act of violence; it was as if night and day had suddenly become inter-changed.

Dexterity of hand, strength, a cool head, and cool blood when required, these were every bit as good as wisdom gained from books, or inherited businesses. Some fellows who had never set foot in 24 Krakovska Street, except to attend one of the socials, had become rich without the slightest effort on their part.

Only why, why, for God's sake, did it have to be here, in this cellar of all places? He thought again of a little boy in a sailor suit whom he had seen in the park. Dita had told him once that she'd worn a dress with a sailor collar when she was a little girl.

Neugeborn was not impressed by the vaulted cellar where he sat perched on the files of people who were no longer alive. He didn't like buildings that had been spared by the Office of Architectural Monuments. From the standpoint of his locksmith's craft, they just meant a lot more work. The corridors here re-minded him of old people. He pushed away the thought of how much effort it took to go back to his workbench now that he knew there was a simpler way to get to the top. And in a store, after all, who asks questions about the currency you pay with?

Sometimes there were parties in the Jewish Religious Commu-nity building. There was a piano in one of the rooms on the ground floor where the guests from Lublania and Krakovska, along with other young people from Prague, could dance to the latest tunes. Twice the Community gave Chanukah parties, and the organizers were pleased that over 500 people came and the only people who looked as if they weren't enjoying them-selves were the fire prevention squads.

There were always a few people to be found who tried to glue together old and new traditions, contributing operatic arias that seemed somewhat exotic to the young people, and folk songs that sounded old-fashioned, and other songs they'd resur-rected that didn't mean much to anybody.

But because the kitchen and the service usually functioned to everybody's general satisfaction, nobody went into unnecessary detail about how the blood of animals designated for slaughter and for food represents their souls and that, therefore, according to Jewish regulations, it should be removed from the animal before its meat is prepared for eating.

Once the old chief rabbi made a nice speech about trees, as if it were trees that gave birth to life—or at least dry earth in a fresh and living forest. And about how for centuries Jews have been planting trees in gratitude—a cedar for a son, a cypress for a daughter. It reminded Fitzi of the legend of how people are not allowed to eat from the tree of life and still live forever. Probably nobody ever did either, he thought to himself. Not during the last few years anyway. A person can afford to be pontifical only now and then, and never for very long. But who eats only from the tree of paradise and not the fruits of all the other varieties of perversity?

When he'd been there the last time, they'd just been lighting the eighth candle on the menorah. A couple of people had begun to weep.

Suddenly Fitzi drew himself up straight, as if he could see himself. "I'll tell you something, no matter if it sounds good or bad to you," he said aloud. "Right or wrong. I've had things bad for long enough. Very bad indeed. Now I want to have it good. Don't you?"

But he heard her answer. "Good?" she asked reproachfully. "I want it to be absolutely fantastic, Fitzi, and that's the problem." She laughed loudly. "That's more than just 'good' and having your head full of worries. 'Fantastic' means having it good and not needing to worry about a thing."

She was wearing a pink blouse, and a pink kerchief was tied over her hair. Blond hair and regular features, a grown-up smile, and white teeth—straight, except for one that was a little crooked—this was the picture Fitzi saw. She smelled of soap. She was prettiest when she simply smiled and said nothing. He wished she'd ask him to share his days and nights with her.

He'd say yes. Fitzi had exchanged the insecurity of an adolescent for the loneliness of an adult without even realizing it. He understood women only so far as he understood people in general. The idea of a couple—man and woman—was linked in his mind to the image of Adam and Eve. Beyond that, he depended on himself, the way a tightrope walker depends on his sense of balance and on luck. It hadn't failed him yet.

Fitzi was silent, realizing how alone he'd been in the cellar on his nocturnal mission. He realized correctly that she didn't want to have anything to do with it.

Neugeborn thought back to a lecture he had gone to hear with Dita at the I.B.W. library in Mala Karlova Street, "You and the Promised Land." She wore a summer dress. He told her about how often during the war he had calculated the distance between Theresienstadt and Prague. That was where his home was. He multiplied it by how many times it had been taken away from him. He couldn't feel at home anywhere else. And why should he, for God's sake?

Only out of habit he picked up a box of wooden rulers bearing the inscription "U.S. Army. Made in Belgium. 30 centimeters—12 inches," sent by the American organization JOINT, for Jewish children in Prague. Originally there had been fifteen thousand children, but only about one hundred had returned. Dita and he were among them. Children, children. They were not children any longer. He had to shake off the feeling that he was treading on his shadow. He sat down on a heap of files. In the darkness he composed a report (never transmitted) on the state of his soul.

Dita, I love you more than anybody has ever loved anyone before. I wish I could write it out in capital letters so it would shout. There is nothing I have to offer you. Underneath, he wanted to write, *I swear.*

9

By the time Lev Goldblat reached Maislova Street in the Old Town, Neugeborn was already back at 24 Krakovska Street, bundled up in a blanket that had belonged to 53 Lublania. The boys' and girls' hostels helped each other out. The war had not been over very long, so there was still a shortage of things that meant warmth.

Andy Lebovitch had already asked Neugeborn if he got anything from her. He carefully slurred the last words because he knew how fast Fitzi was with his fists.

The snow on the windowsill reflected light into the room. Dreamily Neugeborn scratched his fair hair. His forehead was deeply furrowed. Under the blanket his handsome worried face was shrouded in dimness, like everything, except Andy's last few words. They floated around the room until the gray blue light at the top of the window melted into the whiteness that flushed up from the bottom.

Lev Goldblat got back to Lublania Street and reached over and caressed Isabela's fleshy shoulder. He did it awkwardly. He didn't make anyone much of a lover anymore.

"You can't fool me," Isabela whispered.

The more time that passed, the less certain was the custodian that what he was thinking about in connection with Dita was a reality.

Next morning Lev Goldblat showed his wife the note. She had been sweeping the snow off the sidewalk.

"Good morning," she greeted him, her forehead wrinkled in a frown. "I've saved your piece of fish for you from last night's supper. It's in the kitchen. Only, where you're concerned, night isn't night anymore, or morning morning. You don't have any sunrise or sunset at the proper time anymore. You can't even get a minute's peace and quiet now, can you?"

"Thank you. I'm not hungry just now. Give the fish to your darling cats. You're thinking of them anyhow. Shall I cut yesterday's bacon for the traps?"

The fish lay untouched in its dish between the double windows. The black and ginger bodies of two of Isabela's cats, on the prowl for tidbits, froze into immobility like a double shadow with two varicolored heads. Neither the custodian nor his wife made any move to chase them away. A third cat, dappled like a miniature leopard, rubbed herself ingratiatingly against Isabela's fat legs. Lev Goldblat's anxious eyes, which had been clinging for comfort to his wife's face, dropped to stare at her feet.

"The traps can wait a bit. Your ankles are swollen again," he added after a pause. "That's because you never sit down."

"You ought to go and get your hair cut," answered Isabela. "You look like Esau! I'll tell you the truth, it's a funny business, this is, as funny as any I ever came up against. Best thing you can do is tear the note up." She drew the deep long breath that was habitual with her. Vertical furrows divided her low forehead, and at the temples the black hair grew in twin arcs almost down to her eyebrows.

"Get away with you!" she snapped at the striped cat at her feet. "Go mind your own business!" And then to her husband, in a slightly kinder and more subdued tone: "Lucky for us there's no soup ever eaten as hot as it's cooked."

He looked up at her again, but that one glance was all he could manage. "If anybody wants me, I'll be in the yard." He changed his glasses before he went out for a pair that held more firmly behind his ears and didn't continually slither forward down his nose. He had extraordinarily small ears.

"Tear it up," Isabela said again. "We've all got plenty of time for our cloak of shame. I hate informers, whoever they are, as much as I dislike cleaning silver."

"Who's talking about cleaning the silver?" answered Lev Goldblat. "Who's talking about hot soup?"

To change the subject, he asked her if she had read in the *Jewish Gazette* about the warehouse superintendent from Mukachevo.

"He looked like Max Baer, the world heavyweight champion. Why did he do it? He could have lived to be a hundred."

"He probably didn't have anything to look forward to anymore," said Dita, overhearing them as she came out of the house. "Or maybe going on living took his life?"

"For better, for worse," said the custodian.

Isabela started sweeping the snow off the sidewalk.

Dita had to wait a moment to get through. "What are our Jewish kittens doing?" she asked.

"I'm afraid they're more normal than people are," replied Isabela.

Dita answered only with her dazzling smile. She was dressed in her three-buttoned brown tweed jacket and a peach skirt, a sort of dirndl, with a silk scarf and sweater.

The rest of the fish, in the dish behind the open window, had been steadily disappearing inside black Rita and ginger Sarah. They licked their furry muzzles with small pink tongues, crawled to the edge of the sill, their full bellies touching the white window frame like inflated bladders, and leaped out to the naked branches of a lilac tree.

"When you see Neugeborn, tell him he is crazy," Isabela added.

"Why?" Dita asked. "Having a dog named Hitler isn't, after all, the worst idea in the world."

two

I hate ugliness. Ugly people are the first to die.
—FROM THE DIARY OF A GIRL WHO LEFT PRAGUE FOR ISRAEL

*As long as you have a mother, she will tell you fairy tales
and then you will go on telling them to yourself.*
—A GIRL FROM LUBLANIA STREET HOSTEL

1

The clerk cast a glance at Dita. "A bracelet?" Perhaps he was
thinking she needed a new spring coat instead. "In what price
range?"

"I don't know how much bracelets cost."

The clerk wore a well-tailored gray suit and vest.

The idea of buying a bracelet wasn't a new one, yet she felt
like an acrobat on a thin wire stretched across a busy street.
She chose a bracelet in a corner of the velvet-lined drawer. The
clerk held its clasp between his fingers, and she knew right away
that this was the one she wanted.

"I saw that one here last week in the window," she said.

"Five thousand," he said. "It's a beautiful piece. Shall we try
some others?"

"I think I am going to take this one, except—" She unwrapped
the packet of foil on the counter. She laid her student card
beside it.

"I inherited it from my uncle. He was a dentist," she explained.
"They told me it was twenty-two-carat gold. If this is enough

to pay for it, I'd like to have that bracelet."

He bowed to her. "In the meantime, I'll polish it up for you, if you don't mind. Actually, this sort of thing doesn't happen to us every day, so . . ." He pressed a button under the counter and a bell rang. For a second she was embarrassed. "This is our first case . . ."

A woman emerged from the goldsmith's workshop behind the showroom. The clerk said a number, probably some code.

"May we have a look at your foil?" asked the clerk.

The woman glanced quickly at her and then took the foil and carried it over to a microscope. The clerk looked at Dita.

Since morning she had been thinking about the excursion being organized that summer by the International Blue and White Student Union. According to the *Jewish Gazette,* students would be given first priority.

After four weeks she wanted to get rid of the gold and use her own talents to fish with the same net as the other girls from 53 Lublania did.

"You may have the bracelet," said the clerk, when the woman came back after the foil had been weighed and examined. "If you like, we can pay you the rest in cash. There's a bit left over. Is there anything else you would like?"

"Give me back six pieces of foil and the rest in cash."

"You have lovely blue eyes," said the clerk.

"I want you to engrave something on the inside of the bracelet. It's kind of a motto of mine. It's very short."

The clerk took out a notepad and unscrewed his fountain pen.

"D.S. 3/21/1947," she dictated. "Life isn't what we want, but what we have."

2

Men on National Avenue turned around to look at her. A woman is an elegant animal, as Brita has often said, she thought to herself. My God, I am not so innocent. She passed a pair of lovers, their arms around each other's waists. Some things need no explanation.

She was playing her secret game, imagining someone beside her. There were two of them—D. E. Huppert and Fitzi Neugeborn—whom she imagined most often. But, like Herbert Lagus before them, neither yet represented for her that "green lake" or a "path from somewhere to somewhere else." She thought about them the way girls think about boys when it's just day-dreaming, not consuming passion, and the boys and their roles are interchangeable.

Fitzi cared for her, maybe. But how deeply, and how long was his urge going to last? And where would it take her?

It was a lovely day. The winter had been unusually long, but all at once, one Saturday in March, the sunshine melted all the snow away, the wind turned warm, and suddenly it was spring. On such days—and sometimes on Sundays—she felt something she couldn't express. Then she thought about Lebovitch. Andy, like a bitch, was able to do it with anybody. The way he stuck in her mind reminded her of an onion.

Andy's memory was like a piece of Swiss cheese. He only remembered the good things that had happened to him, no matter where or when or how it had been. Or if he never forgot the worst things, at least he didn't bother other people with them. In Theresienstadt, when he'd been two months short of being sixteen years old, he was initiated into the mysteries of physical love by a twenty-year-old prostitute, a half-Jewish girl who had been with the German circus company "Sonne," working as a bareback rider and helping out as a cashier. Andy claimed an artist had painted her portrait once. He lost track of the girl somewhere in Poland. The painting got lost too, of course, along with the artist. For Andy, she was the most beautiful of all the women he'd ever known. He insisted she looked like Mata Hari and that he was still in love with her. It wasn't only because she'd been so kind to him but also because of what she'd taught him and because she predicted that he'd have luck with girls.

She smiled to herself. Who could you really believe when they were recounting their past?

The carefree irony in his behavior combined with his lack of shyness and an attentiveness which seemed rougher than circumstances demanded had actually brought Andy closer to her day by day, though it was more from admiration than a girl's interest in a boy.

Perhaps Lebovitch figured that he had risen from the dead, so he could permit himself anything where the female half of humanity was concerned. During the selection of children and old folks in Birkenau in the fall of 1944, Lebovitch got as far as the showers. They were ordered to undress quickly and to put their belongings in a pile so the underwear could be disinfected while they bathed. There was a German officer with them who was drunk on vodka, saying that he heard that when the whole world was flooded, the Jews got along because they had learned how to breathe under water for forty days. He was curious to see if they would be able to survive the next five minutes.

Something had gone wrong. The officer ordered the doors opened. He told them to get dressed again. Andy said that before the silence was shattered, you could hear a noise inside the shower heads, like a mouse scratching around up in the ceiling instead of water. Crystals of hydrogen cyanide were being poured into the showers. Then it was like rock crumbling. Or somebody dumping sand in the wind. The tide coming in an invisible sea.

When there was light, Andy had seen gouges in the ceiling from the fingernails of those who had been ahead of them, at the time when there was still plenty of gas. The gouges were rough-shaped stars or strange hieroglyphics no one could decipher.

And when everything was quiet, the most greedy among the Germans started to count the gold and money—hidden and discovered treasures from garments and linings—and the most cynical among the Jewish *Sonderkommando* started counting their smaller prey, and saying their prayers. Andy had arranged the *Sonderkom-*

mando members into three categories: the cynics, the bastards, and the saints.

Ever since that time, he treated everything as if he were going to lose it again in five minutes. It was a pleasure to look at him eating lunch, or supper on Friday evenings when both houses were dining together. He ate fast, as if he were subconsciously afraid that what he didn't swallow immediately he never would. Then in the same breath he'd ask her, "Dita, are you really still a virgin?" Or, "Do you know how to dance a waltz?" Or, "Rats and mice are everywhere. Six million rats."

"When it was dark, we were all like blind rats," Andy said once. "We lived and died like rats." He was obsessed by rats, but he didn't act that way.

For Andy, every meal was a celebration. In this sense, he was a true pagan, appreciating every day and every night for what they were and for the very fact that they *were*. He had his sunny days and his rainy ones, days when snow fell and when the wind blew. He even savored the experience of taking a bath.

She looked around her. It was a friendly street. Just recently there had been snow everywhere, then mud. Suddenly everything was clean, like the springtime itself. At those moments the past seemed to her like last winter's snow, like the mud that was gone, like the spring that was coming. It's true that life is really short, as older people always say.

Now Lebovitch had an elegant thirty-eight- or forty-year-old mistress who "wanted to make up for those terrible years." She was as blond as a Viking and looked a bit German or British. For Andy it was always a delight to look at her face and her white body. He said that in the morning when he opened his eyes, she was already clean and her hair was neat. She paid for him, naturally, out of her husband's income. She made him shirts and promised that for his birthday on the twenty-first of December she would knit him a blue dressing gown that came to his knees and a brown necktie with blossoms, and engrave a pair of gold cufflinks with the initials A. L.

What pleased him most was when she had told him that he

was ever so much better than her husband, as if this were something any married woman would find hard to believe. He claimed that the more experience he had the stronger it had made him. Once he wore a white silky ascot from Italy, and she invited him to a very expensive restaurant, The Two Swans, where reservations for dinner were requested, and told him that in that white scarf he looked like a prince. He didn't know then what to remember first: the perfect order of the meal's courses—snails with garlic in a butter bath, grilled frogs' legs with lemon, and filet mignon, with a glass of Cinzano first, then white wine and later red wine—or her telling him that he was a prince. He almost felt as if he were. "She keeps trying to show me she's no whore," he said.

Dita walked slowly. The sun was shining. The street was quiet. A radio in an open window not too high from the pavement was playing a familiar melody.

For a few seconds Dita pictured Liza's father and sister. She could imagine what Liza's father must have been shouting after working for a week on the *Sonderkommando,* when the Germans shot him right by the wall of the crematorium.

Finally she put a smaller question mark next to D. E. Huppert's name, as if she were giving him a gift. We are just as crazy and not one bit smarter than our ancestors in their leopard skins.

On the way back to the hostel she bought some pastries, cookies, and wine for her birthday party. Bread, butter, ham. Paper napkins. She didn't forget anything. She went into the Fleurop flower shop on October 28 Street and bought an aspidistra. She was very choosy and irritated the salesgirl.

She was glad that she had almost gotten rid of the gold foil. Dragging her heavy burden up to 53 Lublania Street, she smiled as though she had been given all these things as birthday presents. The more her knees tended to buckle under her, the prouder and happier were her thoughts.

"There!" She puffed as she reached the building and put her packages down on the sidewalk for a moment.

She was less preoccupied with her new possessions than with

the prospect of that trip abroad with the International Blue and White Student Union and the promise it held out to her.

She suppressed the pleasure of her new bracelet. And she knew that if she thought of someone tonight before she went to sleep it would be D. E. Huppert.

3

Dita went over to the door and opened it abruptly. She and Tonitchka saw only Linda's back.

"There are things a person kills for," she said. "I tried to find out what happened to our laundry on Josefovska Street and to Grandma Olga's field in Habry near Golcuv Jenikov. Too bad my ancestors never gave me a chance to find out how much poetry there is in the smell of manure. That reminds me, I'm going to need a new bathing suit."

Dita put a record on her phonograph. She knew right away that Brita had stretched her shoes again. Brita's foot was as wide as Dita's was long. Once the Holy Virgin even borrowed one of her skirts; she couldn't get it fastened, so she used one of Dita's safety pins.

"It's fun to pay attention to one's appearance," she said.

"You ought to see how you look!" said Tonitchka, but she thought Dita was pale. Like a girl who leads too active a night life.

"All I want in the near future is to get a place in the I.B.W. excursion to Switzerland," Dita said. "They need escorts for some undernourished Jewish children."

"You speak a little German, don't you?"

"A bit—when I can stomach it. But I intend to take some courses in English and French."

And later, "I read in the papers about an actress who was asked what her greatest wish was. 'To give somebody at least a little bit of happiness every day,' she answered. So they asked what she meant by happiness. She just gave them an unreal smile and didn't say anything. She's got a husband and a child and she's beautiful and famous. There was talk at one time that she had a lover who was happy with her; she brought him roses every day. But he probably got scared away by her devotion. People aren't only scared of petty things, but of big things too. I don't equate big things with money. With a beautiful painting, maybe. Or with some lovely song. I don't know. Maybe I'm a little obsessed with songs, in spite of the fact that Neugeborn thinks it's death I'm obsessed with. When love and bread are in a race, Grandma Luisa used to say, love usually comes in second."

"Do you think about them a lot?"

"Not really."

"I probably wouldn't think about it so much either if the people at work didn't look at me like I was some untamed beast about to wake up any minute."

"I heard they shot that actress's father because he joined the Germans during the war," Dita said. "But after the war she fell in love with a Jewish boy. You know, I'd give a lot to know what it is that attracts one person to another. We'll probably never know why anyone does what he does."

She slipped two sheets of foil each under Brita's and Liza's pillows.

"You're not going to give away gold, are you?" Tonitchka protested.

"They say that money helps man to like reality."

In Tonitchka's admiration Dita sensed an echo of the same fear that had made her wait four weeks to decide whether the foil was really hers.

"If you'd been born a hundred years ago, you'd certainly have had a *von* in front of your name," Tonitchka said, instead of thanking her.

"Apparently that actress wrote beautiful letters to her lover," Dita went on casually. "About how much she loved him and always would for as long as she lived. Things like 'My darling, I'll love you for all my life. I wish you happiness and peace.' And so on. And about how her heart stopped when she thought about him or when she walked through places they'd been together. But she couldn't understand why he hardly ever answered her letters. If I'd been in her place, I think I would have understood."

She looked at the walls with their posters and the map and magazine covers of leggy women posing provocatively while suntanned men in the background smiled at them.

"You lack nothing," Tonitchka said.

"I know, and when I'm old, people'll say how I must have been beautiful when I was young."

"No, really," said Tonitchka.

"When I was a little girl, my mother told me she'd expected me to be dark, with brown eyes and black hair," Dita said with her careless smile. "Mother took me home from the red brick maternity hospital and saw that my eyes were dark and that I had dark fuzz on my head. But my eyes turned blue, and when new hair grew in it was blond. With each new birthday it was more obvious that I was going to be tall and always blond. At first glance Hitler would have been delighted."

Downstairs in the basement Lev Goldblat was making his usual clatter with a mousetrap. Isabela's strong voice penetrated the corridors and the walls.

"In a way, I feel too that I am just as I came from my mother," Tonitchka said.

Dita didn't say anything to that, and went on: "In school I always had to sit way in the back so other kids could see. They say I cried when I was in first grade and I asked the school doctor whether there was some sort of operation to make people shorter. It wasn't much fun either when boys my age ignored me. I used to envy small girls like you because they were usually luckier with the boys."

"Fitzi came to see Linda again. It didn't work out."

"Both fortunately and unfortunately, nobody stole anything on account of me, though he might have wanted to. If I were a real femme fatale, I'd enjoy planning how to lead him astray, but as it is, I'm a failure."

"If you don't do what a boy wants right away, they'll say you just lie in bed like a corpse."

"I don't want to be one of those people who ruin their lives by always wondering what people will say," Dita said.

Tonitchka was small. Dr. Fitz's series of hormone treatments had failed. She had spent her formative years in camps. She tried to make up for what nature and the Gestapo had deprived her of with cheap feminine tricks. She slept with an advertisement clipped from *Women's and Girls' Companion*. "I AM BEAUTIFUL," it said. "I attained the shape of my bosom, an imposing embellishment of my beauty, simply by using Professor Larry's Breast Balsam." She had a boyfriend of sorts who was a typesetter in a print shop on Legerova Street, not far from here. She confided to Dita that he liked to kiss the tattoo on her forearm. Earlier she had followed the lead of Kitty Borgerova and taken a one-day job as a model, and the artists had obviously guessed wrong about her age.

"To Andy, women are like food in a restaurant," Dita said. "He wants it ready-made. He's not interested in what must be done in the kitchen, who does the shopping or cooks or washes the dishes afterward. He wants to eat, pay—or leave without paying—and that's it."

"According to Andy and Fitzi, a girl shouldn't be a virgin forever," Tonitchka said.

"They think sex is like swimming. You have to learn how as soon as you can to keep from drowning in it."

"Fitzi survived eighteen transports and Andy sixty."

"They helped each other like a pack of young wolves. Each contributing the best he could." She thought about when the best was the worst and the other way around. But she didn't say it.

"You want me to wash your hair?"

"Would you like to?"

"Fitzi told Munk that you saved some kids' lives during the war."

"I used to look after a couple of kids in Theresienstadt. That's all."

"Close your eyes so the soap won't sting."

Always aware of her height, she lowered her chin to make herself seem shorter.

"What we have now is a different sort of competition," Dita said. "Tomorrow I will take you to lunch in a nice inexpensive restaurant. Grilled duckling—huge portions. And we will have beer. Why should we eat like beggars every day?"

Tonitchka smiled and kissed Dita.

"Isn't it nice when people like you—especially when you have money?" Dita said. "I've already gotten used to the fact that people it's fun to be with are unreliable, and the ones you can bet your life on are bores."

"What happened next?" Tonitchka returned to a previous conversation about a man from Dita's past.

"I knew what he was thinking. Because I was so grown up, somebody could pick me out for what, in Birkenau, they called 'the massage department.' "

"What happened to him?" Tonitchka asked.

"One day he didn't come," Dita answered.

"I can understand why some people would rather be anything but Jewish."

"You don't look very Jewish."

"You don't look especially Jewish either."

"You have a nice small plain nose."

"You too," Tonitchka said. Eating a piece of bread, she looked into Brita's mirror.

"Isn't that some body?" asked Dita.

Tonitchka swallowed the last morsel, blushed, and stared out the window.

The room smelled of whitewash mixed with DDT and eau de cologne, as well as odors from the pantry, which was made from a packing case with "Phillips" stamped on the side. A rag and scouring powder lay on the floor. Brita had brought the packing case when she came back from England.

"Think what you want," Dita said. "You have to be able to say no. But a person lives as much by day as by night, and everything has its own magic. I think I'd mind it just as much if somebody thought I was a nun, or just the opposite—that I had no other interests anymore."

"Mack the Knife" was on the other side of the record Dita had sacrificed lunch for today. The room sang with the English lyrics. She was thinking about which records to buy to enlarge her collection.

"I've got to be going," Tonitchka said. "There is a French war movie at the Passage Theater, *First After God.* About a ship captain who hauls a couple of hundred Jews around the world. Won't you go with me? What are you going to do?"

"To tattoo my other arm," Dita replied.

After Tonitchka left, Dita went to the bathroom and got undressed. She turned on the bath water and sprinkled a handful of camomile into the tub, then added a few drops of eau de cologne. The steam rose fragrantly. She lowered herself into the water.

She inspected herself closely. Where her breasts began to rise, the skin changed texture within a single millimeter. What can explain the fact that things which are put together again seem, in memory, better than they were to start with? She looked down at her skin as it turned rosy in the water. Long legs with firm thighs. Two supple pads of muscle beneath her belly. Will I always have to depend on myself to get what I want in life? She looked at herself as if she had a hundred eyes, each of which, simply by squinting, could see all the images she'd accumulated in eighteen years.

What I am fighting now is my private invisible war, and it's nobody's business.

It was like being an iceberg afloat in the dark night without any of it being visible above the surface except a sharp summit, and then only occasionally. It was as if she realized her strength and at the same time the reason for her fear. Is it possible that the harder you try to be independent and free the more lonely you feel? How do you suppose people felt during the war who escaped into the forest or hid themselves like submarines in cities—most of them enemy cities?

Sometimes Dita's mother had counseled her to be careful, but it was a different kind of caution than what she'd needed between 1939 and 1945. And it wasn't much use to even the most careful.

She'd told her to be careful about who were her friends and who were just acquaintances, that it's human nature to betray one's friends especially. Finally it turns out that people even forget their good friends and cultivate their enemies simply because friends aren't dangerous, while enemies are. Don't be too easily accessible for anyone, her mother had advised her, and don't let anybody be too sure of you. It's better if even your best friends aren't absolutely sure of you. The strongest of them reject their friends in the end and turn into enemies. That's human nature, and who is any different?

It was not only her body she was looking at and listening to. She was listening to a voice inside her. It gave her the impression of being a person walking on a very fragile surface—like ice on the water in winter.

She found herself judging people by whether or not she would want to be in the camps with them. How would they behave? What would they be like? Was it the impossibility of flying from memory and, with that, from responsibility? I am not interested anymore in fighting for some momentary success, as if there were still some sort of war going on.

She thought of the past and of the extraordinary thread linking everything already seen, heard, and lived through with what one expects of life in the time still to come. She thought about how useless it seemed to try to cut all these threads at once—the ones that tied into time past and those that remained hidden by the veil of the future. What was it that could join the past and present and future into a single moment like this?

The water was pure and warm. It was very pleasant to lie back here. She was very close to herself. She thought about the International Blue and White Student Union and its parties, meetings, and dances, and how she had danced with D. E. Huppert, Lagus, and Neugeborn.

4

As the March night waned toward morning after the party for her coming of age, Dita Saxova had a strange dream. She was with D. E. in some country hotel. D. E. was at the bar, serving beer and tea and coffee with rum to the laborers and draymen and farmers. He was wearing a white apron and checkered pants. Outside, darkness crouched on the windowsill; from inside, yellow light poured out through the glass. It was already late and people were beginning to go home. Finally there was just one person left, a tall fellow with a shock of dark hair. D. E. cleared his throat to let him know it was time to go home. When the man didn't leave, D. E. grabbed the lapels of his khaki jacket, ready to throw him out.

Suddenly a kitchen knife flashed in the man's hand, its blade honed to a fine edge. He held it the way children do when they throw darts. The knife's curved handle with its greenish brass inlay parted the air like the prow of an ancient galleon. D. E. ducked behind a chair.

When Dita glanced at the tall man's face, he stared as if he had swallowed a fish bone and couldn't breathe or call for help. Then she saw that both figures were one and the same person.

A cuckoo popped out of the clock, its glass eyes bulging. Dita wanted to scream but couldn't. A light went on in one of the rooms on the other side of the courtyard.

For a while the dream clung to her like a crumpled dress. It was raining. The drops drummed against the windowpane. The night brimmed with water and darkness. The rain tapped out signals like someone throwing something against the glass, crumbs or sand or coins too tiny to buy anything with. The wind moaned as if in ancient grief.

She leaned back against the bedstead. The bed belonged to her, a gift of the Community's welfare department. It had been presented to her in 1945 because she was one of the girls who had lived the longest at 53 Lublania.

My God! It had been such a nice party. Munk keep reassuring

her: "You've got your whole life in front of you, Dita. Maybe someday you'll look back with longing and envy on the courage you have today, on everything you're living through now." Or, "Just think about what you're doing, girls; think what you're doing!" Or, "Lack of faith is against the law now. That's the right of revolution. Hope is all that's allowed. We don't quite understand it yet, but we know enough already to realize that outlawing hopelessness is a tremendous thing, no matter how ridiculous it may seem."

Liza tossed in her sleep. "Let me sleep," she mumbled. "I've got to sleep."

Dita waited, momentarily distracted. She might give something else away. No . . . silence.

Dita groped around the bed. The bottom sheet was as wrinkled as if she'd wrung it. She looked down at her body in the dim light. Her nightgown was hitched up above her waist. On the night table the new bracelet glittered in its case on top of her underwear. Beside it lay the record Munk had given her for her birthday—"I Love Life." She pulled down her nightgown and closed her eyes. She ran her hands gently over her body, wishing that they were a man's hands.

On other nights when darkness drew its veil over the things that kept people in a state of sober wakefulness all day, she sometimes had dreams of a beautiful white house, of D. E. Huppert and the other boys, or of the fisherman in *The Rat Catcher* who always says today what he should have said yesterday; but these were only repetitions of familiar things and didn't trouble the peace of her sleep.

Aside from the sounds of other people's sleep, the room was quiet. She ran the tip of her tongue over her lips. Remotely, as though it were something separating her from herself and linking them both together, she thought about the connection between a father and a mother and the fates of their children.

The room was small, she could easily see from end to end of it even in this darkness, and she was deeply aware of her two roommates lying so close to her. She had an impulse to touch them and caress them, like a mother caressing her sleeping children. For a few moments she stared at her own hands, stretched out in the dark, waiting for something.

Time passed as if washed away by the rain. The clouds floated away from the window. Still the rain kept up.

It was the weirdest feeling, like drinking sweet lukewarm milk and lying on the bottom of a warm ocean with her eyes open, watching transparent blue and red fish and flowers all around her. She was getting warmer. It was strange, pleasant, and scary. Her hands, feet, and face became tense, her heartbeat, and her breath came faster. Then everything went black. It lasted for five or ten seconds. Finally, like an echo of that blackout, shame crept in. She waited for morning.

Liza slept like a deer with her blanket tossed back. Her arms and legs curled up under her belly. She didn't have much of a bosom. Brita lay in the shade of the new rubber plant, huddled in her bedclothes. One plump leg protruded in three places: ankle, knee, and thigh. It was still raining when dawn came.

Liza woke up first. "God, did someone sell the alarm clock? It didn't go off!"

Brita's underwear had been tossed carelessly around the room and was mixed up with Liza's things. She yawned.

"Is there anything left to eat?" asked Liza.

Holy Virgin began to sneeze. She sneezed seven times.

"Justice," she said. "Why do they say all brides are beautiful?" Her flesh shook.

"There must be some butter left over from last Wednesday," Dita announced.

Brita turned to Liza. "Are you really missing a pair of red panties, you communist?"

"I drove somewhere last night," Liza said.

"Dita went somewhere, too, didn't she?" Brita asked. "It's always better than to do it in Doris Lewittova's style."

Dita flushed. But she had made up her mind not to fight back.

It was no secret that when Brita went out on Saturday dates with one of her countless boyfriends, as an insurance policy she wore panties which weren't exactly clean.

Finally, Dita managed to pull herself together. "My, you are looking beautiful this morning. How much weight have you gained? All your clothes look too small for you these days. How come?"

She walked over to the cupboard where they kept their clothes and pulled a pair of lace-trimmed blue panties from Brita's pile. "Thanks to my golden hair, I figure I'll always manage to find someone charitable."

Brita yanked them away. "They're too small for you. You can have them, Liza."

"I'm afraid I would look too seductive."

"It's only princesses like you two who are scared of it, but that's only after your first disappointment," Brita said knowingly. "In some circles, fortunately, you don't need any introduction. Anyway it really has an exquisite taste, something like bitter almonds."

"That too?" asked Dita curiously.

Discussion of the panties ceased. As Liza fluffed up her pillow, she found the two sheets of gold foil. The same thing happened to Brita.

"Honestly, somebody must be stealing around here," breathed Liza, glancing at Dita.

"Maybe someday I'll surprise you all," Dita said. But as usual she didn't tell them how.

Liza kicked away one of the cats. It was black Crista.

"That cat outlived Hitler," Dita said in her singsong voice.

"Where did you get this?" Liza wanted to know.

"A real lady never asks a question like that," Dita replied. She tossed her white towel over her shoulder.

"Do you have a new lover?" Liza kept asking. "Someone I know? Is he circumcised? Do you believe it's the advantage they pretend it is?"

"Nobody from our neighborhood," Dita responded evasively. "Definitely no one you'd suspect."

"Got a date with David Egon Huppert?" Brita asked.

"Don't you know that I can't even stand him lately?" Dita asked.

The circles under her eyes deepened. Her mouth curved into a smile, as if she were thinking that this would be another day for daydreaming. The sky had cleared. Looking like ancient Lysistrata, she strode off to the bathroom.

5

"How about it?" asked D. E.

" 'Your heart's your trouble, friend,' " Dita quoted. "Is this thing really yours?"

To the admiration of the local chapter of the International Blue and White Jewish Student Union, D. E. Huppert—with some help from friends in the National Reconstruction Fund in Prague—had bought himself a KDF, a German amphibious car, part of General Patton's Third Army's loot in Pilsen. It had been a virtual steal. It had only cost him the equivalent of one month's scholarship money.

Dita leaned back against the cracked oilcloth upholstery beside D. E. She swallowed a question about who might have been sitting there before. "With you, this ride will be very short or very long," she said.

While Linda, his stepsister, was mean and spiteful and boring, D. E. resembled an elegant and voracious little fish equipped to swim in all sorts of water. In school and in his social life his diplomatic talent shone. He had promptly put all the things he'd learned into practice at the International Blue and White Jewish Student Union. After studying the United States Constitution for one semester, he earned a reputation as a future architect of the constitution of the International Blue and White, and maybe someday of some new amendments to the constitution of the World Jewish Congress.

He loved to talk about what interested him, ideas he agreed with, like democracy versus tyranny. He'd already been on free excursions to Belgium, France, and Switzerland, confirming everybody's impression that he was destined to serve the I.B.W. and, later, the World Congress.

He whistled "Stormy Weather." He'd been introduced to the chairman of the World Congress when he passed through Prague, and had been allowed to join the group that was invited for coffee after lunch at the Hotel Alcron.

Dita turned her face to the wind, savoring the pleasure of being asked out on a date again. D. E. had invited her with his customary tact. The wind tossed her hair, and she put on a kerchief.

As he drove past the corner of Lublania and Legerova Streets, Dita pushed away the feeling that she had nobody to depend on but herself. "Just to make sure, drive on by and don't stop, so nobody sees you," she told him. He nodded knowingly.

She couldn't help wondering how much she'd feel like resisting if D. E. confused her with girls like Doris or Kitty or Liza. Liza had surprised everybody at Lublania by suddenly not seeming to care about what she did with her body.

Before D. E. came for her, Dita had let Tonitchka do her hair. Then she tried out her charms on the tavern keeper across the street. Fortunately his wife wasn't there.

"Nothing's wrong with my heart," D. E. told her with a grin. "What about yours?"

An hour later, they were standing at the window of a little resort hotel in a room decked with fresh flowers. A wet spring snow was falling. The silhouettes of slag heaps from the coal and silver mines loomed low on the horizon. There was a smell of clay in the air.

Out in the parking lot, its rear wheels mired in the mud, was the amphibious wartime jalopy that had traveled the equivalent of three times around the world.

6

D. E. stood behind her chewing a peppermint drop. Among his Ten Commandments were no smoking, no heavy drinking, and no late hours. Only his best friends knew how much he loved to sleep. Most of the hours he dedicated to his books for the good of the world were spent in bed. Even at noon he looked as if he'd been cheated out of a good night's sleep.

"Do you want to stay here?" he asked.

"I don't like it when they check up on you in hotels at night," she answered, as if it were important for her to sound more experienced than D. E.

"Don't worry," he said. He began to whistle the Jewish anthem.

"Maybe you won't be able to wriggle out of it." She let the words glide through her teeth like a song.

"I wish I could figure you out."

"It's never like they say it is." Should she tell him she was happy sometimes without knowing why, then unhappy, not knowing why either? She thought back to when she was thirteen, her first flow of blood.

D. E. swallowed the peppermint. He stroked her hair. His fingertips moved across her cheek. She could feel the warmth of his hand.

"Do you still believe in the stork?" He grinned.

"Would you get me some water from the bathroom, please?" Dita asked.

The door was locked. The window was high. No one could see in, and there were curtains anyway. Long white curtains.

She lowered her eyes and looked out the window. She had beautiful eyes, but even when she smiled her grown-up inscrutable smile they looked sad or anxious, and this was intensified by the moonlight.

They sat down on the edge of the bed. She lay back. D. E. sat beside her for a while. Then he put his head in her lap and moved his fingertips in silence across her eyelashes, over the arches of her closed eyes, her lips, the corners of her mouth, and Dita responded to his hand the way cats do.

"The spring's lovely this year," she said.

"It's taken its time."

"I don't like long winters very much."

"I want you to like it here."

"I know you do."

D. E. said nothing. It was in the air, unspoken, whether it was within his power. And how much it was in hers. Instead she said, "Time feels different to me when I'm out in the country lying in the grass."

D. E. smiled. His eyes glistened. There was something else beyond the implications in her words, and it grew stronger the more softly she spoke.

"It's as if every little place, like this room, is a whole world."

Instead of answering, D. E. caressed her.

"I went to buy a new scarf yesterday. A tall, elegantly dressed young woman came into the shop with her mother. The salesgirl asked if she could help them. The young woman said, 'Yes, I'd like to buy a hat for my mother, don't we, Mommy?' That was all, D. E."

She worried whether she didn't smell too much of soap, and yet was proud of it at the same time. D. E.'s hand warmed her. It cupped her forehead, stroking her temples and the roots of her hair.

"It's true when they say life's beautiful," she said. She half closed her eyes. Actually it was the first time a boy had caressed her this way. She could feel his hand on her temples, on her lips, her chin, her throat, as if it were protecting her.

"You can be glad you're not a girl," she said softly.

She thought briefly of Herbert Lagus and Alfred Neugeborn, whose fingernails were always dirty. She surrendered to D. E.'s hand like the cats in room 16 when she was petting them. His hand was peeling something away from her and adding something too. There were many layers to the feeling.

"Night is more dangerous than daytime," she said.

"What makes you think so?" D. E. asked.

"I don't know. Maybe because of the dark."

"I hope you don't believe in demons."

"Do they come from the north?" Dita smiled. "My caveman ancestors certainly believed in them." She paused. "Are you scared of depths?"

"I'm not scared of height or depth. Not even of distance or of aging."

"Sometimes I'm scared of depths, and of silence or loud noise. Like Tonitchka's afraid of all her past fears. She's ashamed of having been frightened, and she's even more embarrassed that she hasn't gotten over it. Sometimes she gets dizzy spells, as if she were standing on the brink of a cliff."

"You or Tonitchka?" D. E. asked carefully.

"Who wants to be around somebody who's scared all the time?" Dita said evasively. "When we're just talking among ourselves at night, we say all sorts of things."

After a while Dita asked, "Would you always know how to be as nice as this?"

A few times she had to shift D. E.'s hand higher on her chest. It was twilight outside the window. D. E. was caressing her now wherever he wanted to.

"You mustn't laugh at me, D. E." When he did not answer, she added, "And you mustn't feel sorry for me either."

She looked for the moon. It hung in the upper half of the window. The stars were clear. D. E. was silent. She could hear the thumping of his heart and his breathing.

"You mustn't do that, D. E."

She knew he wouldn't answer, and she was glad he didn't. She could see into her own soul. And she saw suddenly that he was like a part of her.

"I have nobody to look after me. All I've got is myself," she said urgently.

D. E. kissed her several times on the temples, on her cheek, her mouth, her forehead. His lips were warm and suddenly his hands seemed to be everywhere. She allowed herself to be caressed and kissed but didn't reciprocate.

In June 1945, right after the war, she'd gone for a ride in a jeep with two Russian soldiers. They had all laughed together, as if the world weren't still one big red bleeding scar. They invited her to go into the woods with them. They'd thought she was more grown up than she was. They sat there on the hood of the jeep that had come all the way from America via Murmansk, their feet planted in the heather, and Dita wished that she could put her arms around the whole world and hug it. Sometimes the problem is simply that a person has to believe in something.

Then the two Russians were talking something over between themselves, and she could feel their eyes taking off her clothing. She realized she was about to join all the girls to whom something they hadn't wanted to happen had happened. She slipped down from the jeep and ran into the woods. She could hear their laughter behind her. Maybe she'd been right and maybe she hadn't.

"You can't do that," she heard herself telling him again. Her voice sounded different now. It was no longer like a turtle's protective shell.

"Yes, I can," D. E. replied, firmly, as if there was nothing more to say. "So can you."

"But just a little," she said. "Just a very little bit. I'm not used to it. Maybe I'll learn, but I'm not used to it yet."

She felt like an island no one had set foot on for a long time. She'd stopped feeling guilty. Moonlight gathered in her eyes. The moon was ripe and very white. Her eyes, which had looked tense and anxious, softened. The window hung like a pale rectangle in the darkness and the silence. A baby cried nearby. Then there was silence again, in which the baby's cry had not quite faded.

D. E. undressed her. Then he got undressed himself. She was conscious of her own body, of her heart beating, her wet eyes. She was trembling all over. It was a wonderful kind of tension she'd never felt before. She could feel a twitching in her abdomen. A shiver ran through her body. She helped

D. E. find what he was looking for, to make up for what she didn't know how to help him with yet. Briefly she wondered whether she'd be doing this if her father and mother were there, and she was suddenly afraid of them, a fear beyond the capacity of respect and shyness to transfer itself elsewhere.

She was glad that D. E. knew what he was doing and how to do it. She didn't want to think about his having done it before. He's had lots of girlfriends. But now she was in their place and that canceled everything else out, even though for them it was just the same. (Once he had mentioned Linda in a way that emphasized the fact that they weren't really blood relatives. There had been the suggestion of something in their relationship that instead of bringing them closer had caused a permanent rupture. There were a lot of prejudices involved and other things too.)

"This is the first time in my life I've been like this, David."

He kissed her mouth.

"I'm not scared," she whispered. "Just a little bit."

"Don't be."

"It's a nice way to be scared. I've never been scared before in such a lovely way. Everything happens so fast."

He could feel her trembling. It was as if there were a secret strength inside her that caught and drew him to her. As if her weakness had become a force. But he didn't tell her he couldn't wait any longer. Or even speak.

"I don't want to be alone anymore," she whispered. "I don't want to dream of awful things and then wake up. I don't want to be like those people who've been dead for a long time even when they're still living."

"You're not alone," he told her.

"And don't tell me this is all I'm good for, David. Never tell me that!"

They whispered to each other from inches away, and she ran her hands caressingly down his back. He told her she didn't need to worry, that everything was all right.

"It's like you're taking me where I've wanted to go for a long time, David." She could feel her head turn as if consciousness were draining away and something quite different taking its place.

She felt the tautness of his skin, and she felt the muscles underneath. When he was dressed, it wasn't obvious how solidly he was built. He lay on his side and drew her toward him.

"No, David, no," she said, all acquiescence, even as, with a whisper, she touched his body. A little while later she was silent and arched in pain. She took D. E.'s body into hers as if he were bread and she was dying of hunger. D. E. went very deep. She wanted to pull away, but he held her too tight and she moved forward as though he'd shot her with an arrow that drew her toward him.

"David!" she whispered, trembling the way her voice trembled. "My love."

"I'm sorry," D. E. whispered.

"Darling," she repeated, still trembling. "I've never called anybody that before."

Then she whispered, "You don't have to be sorry, David. There's nothing to be sorry for. Not to me."

It was like an undeveloped photograph emerging out of the darkness, taking shape as you looked at it, revealing undefined intuitions, transforming darkness and light and making them take on new meaning. It was like a reward for all those who surrender what they will never have again, when giving becomes the same as receiving.

She heard the echo of a choked cry, as though a crumb of pain or joy had caught in her throat, in that narrow passage through which her voice slipped now into a dark and muffled sob, half mad with the gladness of release. It seemed to her that she and D. E. had had a brief and sweet epileptic fit, a bewildering attack. Is that how life begins? Or how it ends? And then she smiled.

It was like when Lebovitch, who had been so close to it, said that when you're dying you feel a sweet, almost dizzy sensation, a marvelous spinning almost like fainting, as if you were escaping from life like air from a balloon. D. E. kissed her. He told her things nobody else had ever told her.

She looked up at the ceiling and felt at peace, moved by something she couldn't specify. It had nothing to do with present, past, or future, and yet it was connected with all three of them. Suddenly she felt larger than time, connected with everything.

She felt a quiet force, something in her that also abided in trees and rocks and the sea, binding her to the whole universe. It was deeper than her conscience. It had little in common with her old experience. She felt something against her thigh, a warm trickle of blood, her body, his body, the strength from his body.

"I know who I am. And I know that I *am*. From now on, everything will be different."

7

But a little later, she felt as if a tide were ebbing. It was almost eight-thirty. Thoughts passed through her head, and it was as if she were somebody else or as if she had two brains, taking note of everything about D. E. that she wouldn't be able to get used to.

It was just a passing thought. Or maybe a way of keeping other thoughts under control. Before, she'd thought of D. E. as an extension of her own body; now it was the other way around. Man and woman. She was tired and it felt good. D. E. handed her a towel, and she held it to herself.

She wished he'd reach and touch her again so he'd notice the bloodstains on the sheet. But she didn't want him to turn on the light.

"I can imagine there are women all over the world who are smiling at the same time for you," she said.

The sky was beautiful. It was dark, as heavy as a reclining woman, veined with silver, breathing many shades of green. The stars were like distant airy ships moving through eternity, from one to the next, forever and ever, a kind of immortality she couldn't explain.

The shadows on the moon looked like canyons and oceans. She thought about the ocean. She didn't know why. The moon looked like a pearly landscape or as if it had leaked out of another sky which was far above it. Sometimes the moon looked red. Or did it only seem that way? Am I different than I was an hour ago?

"I've never seen the ocean," she said.

D. E. eyed her quizzically.

"Do you think I'm crazy for not telling you anything before?"

D. E. still didn't say anything. He was silenced by what she'd said earlier about being here for her mother, for both her grandmothers, for women she knew and for those she'd never even met—so she could collect a share of pleasure and satisfaction on their behalf too.

"Time puts a haze over everything that's happened. But some things, even seen from a distance, probably seem clearer with time than when they were close," she said.

"Maybe," D. E. responded.

"I'm choosy," she said after a while. "I want things to be like they are now for a long time."

"I guess we're both choosy," D. E. said, smiling. He observed his own body. He looked happy and satisfied.

"Sometimes it's enough to know you are with someone who understands and then you don't need to say a thing," she said.

She told him about the girls with her in Poland in 1944 who had been shipped off to the Arctic Sea that summer. "I've always been better off in the end than those I used to envy at first. I've also learned not to overestimate anybody. Or underestimate them either. And that you have to reconsider the values you held yesterday and exchange them for today's values, and the same tomorrow, as circumstances change. Nobody knows who they'll need or when, or who will have to pull them out of the mud. I know what the most important things are in life—food and health and friendship. Because it can't always be joy and fidelity and beauty. But they're the things that give it all sense, even though there's always something missing."

D. E. waited for her to go on. Sometimes it was hard to follow the logic of Dita's words.

"Everybody said the girls were lucky, that they'd be put on some fishing crew," she went on. "They were hand-picked girls, the prettiest and the strongest. They'd been making fish nets out of women's hair in a factory. They did wonders, really—children's clothing, insulation for German army barracks and for the electric stoves. They made riding crops and whips for the lion tamers in Zirkus Busch. And dainty little quirts for the SS *Aufseher*. Quilts and sleeping bags and overalls for German submarine crews. Some of the girls still had long hair when they came to Birkenau. Germans were fussy about having their mattresses stuffed with blond hair, while others preferred children's black or brown curly hair. Or red. Others liked a 'Jewish mixture.' "

"Must have been fun," D. E. said. "I can imagine how you looked without hair."

"I went to the delousing station twice a month."

"Was it far from your barrack?"

"Not too far."

"Did you ever work in one of those factories where they processed hair?"

She laughed. "No. I tried to get out of work as much as possible. Although I know Munk's whole collection of sayings about why a person ought to work so he won't feel like a thief. All I did was haul stone at the Buna Werke. I was afraid they'd send me to work in the soap factory or the candle factory. I couldn't get used to the idea that my Grandmother Olga might be in one of those cakes of soap or candles. Even though some girls produced some very nice perfume and after-shave. If you didn't know what it was made of, it would never even occur to you. Anyway, the perfume was only for women inside Germany, and the soldiers and officers probably didn't care. Maybe the women felt just as elegant as the ones who got French or Belgian perfume from the occupied territories. After all, you can get used to anything."

The dark blue sky, swimming with stars, flowed in through the window. It was a luminous, sweet-smelling evening. The room was still. All you could hear was the fire crackling in the white tile stove.

"I can imagine it," said D. E. after a while. "I'm trying to see it in the right way. I mean upside down."

" 'He who is merciful to the cruel will be cruel to the merciful,' as the rabbis say."

"I know. And, 'It is forbidden to have mercy upon a fool.' "

There was a hint in his words that they ought to forget about it. Or that the world they were living in now was far removed from all that. That things were different now. And that they would be different more and more, every day and night they grew older.

"Why don't you ever talk about it? Don't you want to?" Dita asked.

"Maybe I'm ashamed of it," said D. E.

"We're all probably ashamed."

"There are lots of things I've thrown overboard once and for all," said D. E. without even telling her what they were.

She could imagine. "I guess I must be awfully spoiled. There's something always missing for me in everything. I wish I could be at least half as content as I look."

"They say that in hell false prophets are chopped up for kindling, that frauds and panders sizzle like hot pitch, and that infidels and heretics lie in graves of fire. I guess there won't be anything but ice left for me, as a traitor to my country and king." It was obvious that he'd at least peeked into Dante.

She stretched, smiling, her fresh skin the color of a ripe peach. Her face was long and oval, and her blue eyes looked happy and contented. "People who betray someone's hospitality have it worst of all," she said. "I'm going to be careful not to burn myself on the ice."

When D. E. looked at her questioningly, she continued. "Munk told me about an old Chinese opera where somebody murders the father of this prince and he hires two servants to perform a single duty—to remind him every morning, as soon as he wakes up, of who killed his father and how they did it."

"I suppose the second servant was to tell him good night."

"We haven't had our last word yet, any of us."

"Sure. What is, is, and what is to be will be."

"I see you still keep looking back two years," D. E. said at last. "Try looking ahead two years."

She laughed. "Two years? A hundred years ahead! All right, sure. We only live once."

Then she said, "Have you read the latest *Jewish Gazette?* The Prague Jewish Community wants somebody to run the kosher restaurant, even part-time. They're looking for a waitress too. Good working conditions." Her eyes clouded with imagination.

D. E. was pleasantly self-confident. It was something else that was unpleasant.

"At the same time you were there, I worked in the D.A.W., Deutsche Ausrüstungswerke," he said, as if he were putting a period at the end of a sentence. "Isn't it a lovely evening?" he asked.

"I probably wouldn't talk about it to anybody else, D. E." When those girls left, they really behaved as if they were going to some seaside resort. Some of them had worked in other kinds of establishments than those that processed hair. They were called masseuses. They did all sorts of things with Poles and German officers and enlisted men, with prominent Jewish prisoners who had access to food, not to mention gold teeth and dollars and English pounds. But as soon as they loaded them into the trucks, the girls started getting nervous. Finally they didn't even ask where they were going, just who was sending them there. "In 1944," she went on, "people would probably have found it difficult to go to heaven if there were Germans escorting them. And none of us wanted to make it more difficult for them. You know how an animal must feel when there's a forest fire or a bad storm's coming."

"I didn't know what a sense of humor you had."

"I didn't know it about you either."

"Somebody told me you were raped in the woods somewhere toward the end of the war or right afterward," said D. E. suddenly, in the same tone as when he'd been talking about where he'd worked during the war. "Or almost, anyway," he added.

"You must know best that nobody raped me." Dita laughed mildly. "What they don't say about people! And if it were true, so what, D. E.?"

D. E. smiled back at her. The mildness of her answer had surprised him. He was glad to confirm this, of course, even though he didn't overestimate its importance.

"I know they say that about me, though. They say it about all of us. It's always the same silly story. Two men at least, one standing with a pistol in his hand aimed at your head, finger on the trigger, while the other one does as his heart desires." She shrugged. "That isn't the worst that can happen to you, believe me. Some things that happen you can forget about. Things you can't compare to sickness or death. When you imagine how lovely it would be not to be alive. In comparison to that, what's rape? Whether there are two or three at once? The world's full of all sorts of perversity. It's always just one side of life, D. E."

She smiled just as mildly as she spoke. She was glad D. E. kept silent, stroking her hip. But he did it as if trying to make sure that it was really her, the girl he'd made love to a while ago.

Somebody opened the window from the kitchen below. They could hear the noises of pans and china. It was the dinner hour.

"You're probably the first person I've said that to." She smiled a trifle sadly. "You think I lied to you, don't you?" It sounded as if it were coming from nowhere. She knew she was capable of lying. And that she probably would. She tried to stretch out as comfortably as possible on the bed.

"Do you know this joke?" she asked. "A man comes home from work and gets a telegram. He opens it and reads that his wife, away for a cure at a resort, has died. He folds it up, puts it on his night table next to an alarm clock, and thinks to himself,

When I wake up in the morning that'll be some surprise!"

D. E. looked at her. They heard the noise of tin and glass mixed with the gurgle and splash of dishwater, and for a moment it sounded as if a stack of plates had been shattered. The sound of running water changed into someone's smile. There must have been an older woman in the kitchen.

After a moment D. E. told her, "In a way, everything bad was good for us at the same time. The main thing is to stay alive."

"Now I know what the difference is between us, D. E. You want to live fast and I wish I could die fast. But now I want to live slowly."

"I know just what you want," said D. E. "But besides wanting to live fast, I want to live a long time too. I think we understand each other. Anyway, I hope I understand you. I'm also for anything that shortens a person's suffering."

"Does your formula apply to people too?" She was thinking how unpleasant it was to lose. The way defeat could follow a person like his shadow. You tried to run away, to keep at least a few jumps ahead of it.

"Especially to people."

"But you've already seen the ocean, and you don't ask unnecessary questions. Just to make sure, you collect things that can't be taken away from you. But maybe it's impossible to live fast."

"I do the best I can."

"Tell me what the ocean's like," Dita said, instead of asking why so many people treat life as if something terrible might happen at any second, in spite of everything, and as if the war weren't reliably over yet. Still, wasn't she the first one to react in just that way herself? She looked into the mirror at her body and face. Her last weapon was her smile.

"A place called Biarritz," D. E. said. "We were there just briefly." He was watching her body and face. "We had one of the International Blue and White meetings there. The weather was wonderful. We lived in a nice hotel. In fact, we lived like lords. That won't happen to me ever again. That doesn't matter.

I probably couldn't stand it for too long."

"Were there lots of lovely suntanned women in beautiful bathing suits?" She didn't repeat what she had heard yesterday from old Fatty, about those ninety-three girls of the Jewish School in the Warsaw Ghetto in '43—was that the date? She didn't tell that they had chosen to kill themselves rather than to be selected and sent to the German bordellos.

"There were women there, and without their husbands," D. E. said. "But there was a shortage of the kind who don't scare me."

"What kind of women do you fear most?" Actually she was thinking about those he liked most. It was as if she said "Next time" to somebody who told her that maybe there wouldn't be a next time. Then a third voice insisted that there would always be a next time.

"The ones who are the most willing," D. E. said.

"May I apply that to myself?"

"Only good things about present company," D. E. said casually, and smiled. "These sheets smell good."

"Am I weak or strong, D. E.?"

"You're perhaps both. Why do you ask?"

"You know, when those girls were shipped off to the Arctic Sea, everybody said how lucky they were. But good luck can't take care of everything. Nobody ever saw those girls again. Not one of them."

"We know all that. Why talk about it?" D. E. asked her. "The Arctic Sea, the fishing crew, the fish nets. As far as that goes, the Baltic Sea's not going to see me very soon. Although it's not the Baltic Sea's fault."

D. E. held her head in his lap and caressed her lashes and eyelids and the corners of her mouth.

"What's wrong?" he asked after a while, and then he seemed to sense that he shouldn't have referred so bluntly to whatever it was that had happened.

The sound of music began rising from downstairs. There were only a few musicians, and it sounded cozy.

"It'll be great when you speak English, French, and Spanish or Italian fluently," he said. "Or even a little. You'll be proud of yourself."

"When those girls went off to the Arctic Sea, they were loaded into Mercedes and Renault trucks; those were the best," she said. "Those trucks always reminded me of horses. When the girls started singing, we thought our ears were deceiving us. Maybe the girls were singing because they were glad to be going away or maybe they sang the way people do when they're scared of being alone. It was a beautiful song. About ash trees and mountains, about life and love and everything that only lasts a little while. It's awful, because it could be so lovely, couldn't it? It was as if they were telling the Germans in that song that *this* was their world, not the camp. That the camps belonged to the Germans' world. And that they were glad to be leaving, no matter what the price. We were surprised that they were allowed to go on singing. Then I realized I was crying. I'd been proud of how tough I'd become. Yet all of a sudden tears were streaming down my face because of that song and who was singing it. Then the trucks drove away. There were wild geese or swans flying across the sky. Higher than the chimneys, than the smoke and the barbed wire and the bins above the showers. The geese were flying very high, far beyond all the mess we had to live with. The geese were flying in a strange wedge formation heading south, just the way they'd done last year and a thousand years ago and as they'll probably do ten thousand years from now. Somebody pointed up at the wild geese and said they were a sign of good weather for the girls' voyage. But all I could see were those wild geese getting smaller and smaller until they were just white dots in the sky growing tinier and darker until finally they disappeared. I cried and it was awful, because the people I was with kept going off somewhere and there I was, alone again, the way I'd had to go away from lots of other people, leaving them alone too. And yet that same awful world seemed beautiful to me. I could never explain it. You know I never talked about bad things. Really bad things.

What's the secret life has hidden inside itself? It was like a magnet drawing you toward anything that was alive. Suddenly I felt there wasn't any secret. None at all. Life is what we all have in common. Life is also what's beyond the chimneys; the sky is soft and blue and so beautiful it hurts. That nobody should take possession of somebody else's life, because when you do you destroy your own life too. Because just as you can't have two hearts, nobody can bear another life besides his own. I saw that people could live like animals, but they have another alternative too. So I said to myself that if I had to die I hoped it would be at a moment like that when the roar of the truck motors was dying away and wild geese were flying across the sky."

A shadow of fear or of echoes of fears long forgotten or freshly suppressed, of recognition, and of a kind of admiration passed over D. E.'s eyes. He didn't know if it was only sadness that he sensed in her, or also some will for life: something that can never be explained, never be satisfied, and brings proportionately less to anyone the more he remembers and the more he expects. It was perhaps a sort of happiness or satisfaction that doesn't come only from joy or memories but exists anyway, if only as an illusion.

"It smells like apples here," he said. "I'll bet there're lots of apple trees around. You can smell honey too. Do you like apples and honey?"

"My mother used to eat that on the Jewish New Year so the whole year would be just as sweet."

"So did my parents, and each of us had to take a bite."

"My uncle was in the *Sonderkommando*. He took care of teeth."

"One of my cousins was in it too," murmured D. E.

"Do you know anything about it?"

"I don't really want to," D. E. admitted.

She wondered, only for a second, what she was trying to convince him of, and what it was she was trying to convince herself of. Was a lost virginity enough to allow her to find out everything she didn't comprehend until now? Everything about her life: those quiet, never fully discovered mysteries? Who she is, who she was, and who she will be? And what is life really all about? Was she trying to grasp all at once the motives of her past, of her present actions, and of her future—to grasp it all through one touch?

But she didn't say a word for a while and looked content. D. E. kept silent too.

Dita looked at him. She saw him very close. But was he really so close?

"Every day reminds me of a lottery ticket," she said. "Every day, every hour, every year. Everything."

"Isn't it nice," D. E. said carefully, "that we all have the right to be considered innocent until proven guilty?"

"You don't have to tell me lies. Although I know no man's ashamed of all the lies he tells to girls."

D. E. laughed, and then he dozed for a while. When he woke up, she was still next to him, and he discovered that he'd only slept for a few seconds.

8

From outside they could hear horses running. Then the sound disappeared. They could guess what was going on in other parts of the house. From the nearby village they heard the bells announcing vespers. The wind brought the sound closer and mixed it with the sound of cars on the road between the castle and monastery that had brought them to the inn. They were no more than nineteen kilometers from Prague.

"You really do have beautiful blue eyes," said D. E.

"Arctic Ocean," she said ambiguously.

"And you've got such lovely, gentle eyes," D. E. said.

She took D. E.'s hand in hers and moved it to her heart. Then she kept silent. Her insistent voice had built itself around her like a wall or a bastion, and he suddenly realized that behind that wall was her secret. Perhaps she didn't know about it. Maybe it was better for her not to know, it occurred to him. It was only a tiny idea. The abyss was no less awful just because he

knew about it, or because those big soft blue eyes were sometimes derisive and adult. There was also the hardness that had
been there at first, together with the gentleness, as if there were
no boundary between them.

His hand remained limp. The room was quiet, like deep water
that looks dark simply because it's such a long way from the
surface to the bottom and because the sun has long since set.
Beneath that deep water there was a strange, undiscovered life
she had merely touched, not only her experiences but images
she couldn't throw away or sink like pebbles. Her own dreams
of men and dependability and equilibrium.

"Isn't it how you thought it would be? Is it worse than you
expected, David? Am I even more inexperienced than you
thought I would be?" He was silent. But it wasn't words she
yearned for. She just wanted to hear a voice.

"Do you feel all right?" D. E. asked.

"How about you?"

She got up and walked to the window and looked out at the
stars. She wanted to tell him about a nursery rhyme with stars
she remembered from when she was a little girl longing for
something she herself didn't know. Instead she said, "I know
exactly what I want to do with my life, D. E. First English and
French, then Spanish and Italian. Then a little money, and later
a lot of traveling."

It was always a fight between modesty and unbridled imagination, she decided. Downstairs they were playing a Gershwin med-
ley.

"I wish we could stay here all night. Time's probably much
more important, or at least different, for a woman than it is
for a man. Who knows why? It's perhaps one of the real differ-
ences between women and men." She didn't want to talk about
death anymore. She wished she could talk about whatever it
was he valued most in life.

"You know, when life's as beautiful as it is right now, I'm
not at all scared of dying," she said, almost whispering.

"Do we have to talk about death so much?"

"Perhaps love is like death in a way too, D. E. Maybe love is a kind of sweet death, like babies falling asleep—gentle, innocent, and very fragile. Why does it all remind me of death, D. E.? Am I abnormal? What does it mean to be in love?"

D. E. smiled and closed his eyes for a while.

"Once I was in the women's camp near the Gypsy barracks, where you and Neugeborn and Andy Lebovitch were," Dita said. "We could see the oven from there. There was a sixteen-year-old girl and her mother with me. The mother aged awfully during those seven or ten days. It seemed almost sure they'd take her in the next selection. Because I slept just across the aisle from their bunk, each night I could hear the girl reassuring her mother. But she talked as if it were going to be the other way around, and the mother kept telling her how we've all been born and we all must die, that when life's as miserable as it was there it's really a relief to die, that it wasn't just false comfort. They said nothing about God, even though at night I sometimes thought I heard the old woman repeating words over and over, the way you say your prayers. Then the selection came and the girl kept on telling her mother that there was nothing to be afraid of, that she'd go partway with her. You know, the worst thing about it—and the best thing, too—was that they did select the mother, and the girl was allowed to walk partway with her. As we both know, it could easily have been the other way around. So off they went, both of them knowing that the mother knew she'd never see another sunset. It all looked so calm and peaceful. They'd reconciled themselves, you see? The girl kept her arm around her mother's neck, trying to press her cheek to hers, and they weren't even crying. They just walked on, and it was as awful and as fine as a person can be, and when they got to the gate by the fence the mother simply caressed her daughter's cheek and the girl didn't cry. She looked at her mother soberly and sweetly, probably not wanting to make it any harder for her. And the mother must have felt the same way. So they stood there looking at each other and we watched them, pretending that we did not care. It was more comfortable for both sides.

The girl quickly kissed her mother on the lips and patted her arm, and the mother gave a little smile and winked, and so did the girl. Maybe she told her that dying isn't so terrible, that they'd meet again somewhere, as if she were taking her mother to the railroad station to catch a train and she herself couldn't go any farther than the platform. The way we can know that we're alive and that someday we'll die and that there are worse things in the world."

"What would you like me to do to you?" asked D. E.

"I wish that I weren't afraid of death, even if life weren't so beautiful—you know what I mean? Could you caress me like that some more?" And then she said, "Do you think that we can learn how to die? Learn how to accept, when our hour comes, what is inevitable, whatever it might be? It's an art, for sure, only there are no rehearsals. Your part can be shown only once. Perhaps it takes all a person's talents, just as art does, but more than that, it also takes courage and a sort of dignity. I really don't know. I knew many people who *did* know how to die, and many others who were very, very inexperienced."

D. E. didn't answer. She felt his hand on her hip. It was like a role in a play. She had only heard about it, and now she loved playing it too.

"I'd like to think about the past the way you do," she said. "In fact, I'd like to do everything the way you do. You know, when I'm not doing anything, in a day or two, or even within a few hours, it's like I'm burning inside. Like a house on fire. But instead of trying to put it out at once, I think about how to do it in the best possible way, and in the meantime the house is burning down." She smiled. "I have great plans at least."

"As you see, I don't have blisters on my heels just because my something-great-grandfather fled from Egypt two thousand years ago across the burning sand," D. E. remarked. "And my arms aren't aching for Grandpa either, even though Mr. Chmelnicky hung him with horseshoe nails on a gate somewhere in the Ukraine or Poland."

"It's only the tip of my finger," Dita said. She realized that no person in the world can order or force somebody else to feel what he feels, whether it's pain or joy or expectation or all of them. She was afraid she was boring him.

He smiled and kissed her lips. His breath still smelled of peppermint. He glanced at her. It occurred to him she wasn't as naked as she looked or as she'd acted at first.

"I think they're wrong," she said, "when they say that because of Birkenau the nature of everything has changed, from the core of our earth out to the farthest star, from the trees that were growing before we were born to the babies who haven't come into the world yet. Nothing's changed. Something has simply been added. Something we've all got to learn to live with."

He remembered how they had gone to hear *Eine Kleine Nachtmusik* and how the tears had come to her eyes. How tall and elegant and striking she had been, pleased to have so many of her friends see them together at the concert.

She gazed up at the stars for a few moments without saying a word.

"Everybody talks about stars, as if stars could know what's going on here with us," D. E. said. "I don't ask for anything. I don't know them and they don't know me." He smiled as if he were sure he'd impressed her. She didn't know.

"Tell me some more about your trip to the ocean."

"We left Paris at night. The train looked like a rocket. A sort of flying synagogue. If it hadn't been so expensive, it would have been great. But the International Blue and White paid for the whole thing from start to finish, except for the booze."

"How does it feel crossing the frontier?"

"Strange."

"Sometime I'd like to go with you on a train like that."

"Actually, I like express trains. Do you want me to turn on the light?"

She didn't reply, because she'd expected him to say something else, so he too was silent, realizing it was better to say nothing.

"Everything here's naked," she said. "Does everything look so terribly naked to you too?"

"It's just the two of us who are naked." He laughed and looked at her quizzically. "We didn't just discover that we've got bodies, did we?"

"You're nice and tall," she said. "You know, when I'm with some people, I like myself more, and when I like myself I also like other people. Funny, isn't it?"

"I can't remember when I didn't like myself," D. E. said flatly.

The band in the garden restaurant below took a break, and you could hear the wind, the springtime rustling of the trees, the sound of the forest in the distance, and silence. She couldn't understand that what attracted her to D. E. repelled her at the same time.

"You're grown up in every way, I see, David. How many times have you been grown up like this?" She didn't wait for an answer. "I think I'd like to have a baby. But only with someone who can understand everything that's happened. Do you remember, D. E., when you were in our room one Friday and you brushed against me and I told you not to get me mixed up with someone else? Were you really offended that time?"

"A little bit, but not too much."

"Is it always just 'a little bit, but not too much' with you?" He looked at her.

"Do you think a lot about gratitude too—for what and to whom? What is really a sin? Perhaps I spend too much time thinking about what sin is. I feel one of my usual crazy spells coming on. We call it 'diarrhea of the soul.' "

"Where did you get that bracelet?"

"I'm not all that poor. And sometimes I want to show it. You can't say you've seen me here with nothing on."

In the darkness D. E. laughed. She could feel his hips and muscles and thighs. "I didn't know you could be so gentle and so strong."

"Is that some more of your 'soul diarrhea'?"

"Can I tell you later? Stroke me some more. Nobody ever knew how to caress me as you do. Maybe you were born for me and I was born for you, D. E. I'm not talking about how long it's supposed to last."

"Why do you keep on using my initials?"

"I'm not exactly fond of your stepsister and I don't want to be reminded of her here."

D. E. sighed.

"Her boss is one of those people we were talking about," Dita said. "The side that's lost. They call her 'Gestapo' because she hires Jewish girls and is mean to them. You wouldn't believe it. She's a German Jewess."

For a moment the silence was like a pleasant strange stream running somewhere else.

He sighed again. She changed places with him. He looked strong and calm. She did everything for him that he had done for her. It seemed natural. Once again she observed how strong and clean he was. At 53 Lublania a girl heard about everything. She no longer wondered whether her mother had done this too, and her grandmother; and if she'd ever have a daughter, whether she too would do it. She took him into her mouth.

Later she whispered, "D. E., do you know how to say 'blood' in Italian? *Sangue.* I learned that from Liza. For all that we girls have."

But there was something about it all he didn't understand. A hint of something she still had on her mind. It sounded either as if she'd wanted something and hadn't gotten it, or else as if she wondered whether it were possible to offer someone her own life, as if it were a sunbeam a child tries to catch with his hands. Or wasn't she asking for too much by wanting *everything* right from the start?

"Are you talking to me or to yourself? How does it sound in French?"

Then D. E. slept again for a while, holding her around her shoulders and with his leg over her legs. It was very clean and sweet and innocent. Dita was watching him and she felt the real weight of his body, his hands, his head, his breath, and his hair. She waited, quite still, and then she said, "It was my body and it still is, D. E. Everything's like it was, only better, God! It's all right, David. I guess there's always a conflict between body and soul. The darkest and the loveliest of all temptations. Maybe like everything you pay for with blood. You're afraid of getting too close, and yet at the same time that's just what you want. Is my head too heavy? I wouldn't be here if I didn't want to be, David."

Slowly, so she wouldn't misinterpret it, he got up and went over to the sink.

"You're nice not to turn on the light," she said.

Her eyes loomed large in the moonlight. Her face and lips were smiling, but her eyes stayed grave. D. E. washed himself. When he turned, it was to give her a friendly smile.

9

The resort hotel had been built before the war. It was of brick and stone. Downstairs, cars honked as they came and went, chickens cackled, and a dog barked—a mixture of town and country noises, with interludes of silence. D. E. opened the window, letting in a breeze that carried the smell of forests and fields and of food, along with fresh whitewash from the barn that the hotel owner had turned into a garage.

It wouldn't take long to feel at home here. Somewhere in the distance horses whinnied.

"We could come back tomorrow and go riding," said D. E.

"You know how to ride?"

"A little. Do you?"

"I learned last summer. It's marvelous. It's free and fast and scary."

"It's not much fun to fall off."

"Luckily I never did. If we could stay here sometime, I'd love to go riding with you, David."

The hotel signboard leaned against scaffolding: HOTEL ASTORIA/NOVAK, FORMERLY YELLOW STONE INN. A garden stretched off toward the woods, and there were fields with rows of apple, cherry, and pear trees and gooseberry bushes along the fence, which was invisible now in the darkness. On the other side birch trees tossed in the wind. The trunks of the trees in the orchard had been whitewashed halfway up.

The room was cozy and warm. D. E. put more wood in the

stove—cherry or oak or birch? Amid the kindling were old shingles that caught fire immediately, casting sudden slivers of light over the room.

"Fire can be beautiful too," Dita said. "Can't it?"

"I hope you'll skip the ashes." D. E. grinned.

"How come you're so smart?"

More logs and kindling lay on sheets of old newspaper, away from the fire. Drops of sap beaded on one of the logs. NUCLEAR STORM OVER NEW YORK. END OF AMERICA'S ATOMIC MONOPOLY. ALARM IN THE WHITE HOUSE. The yellowed edges of the paper looked like old parchment. It was all very peaceful.

"D. E.?"

"I can open the other window, if you want me to."

"How did you know that's what I wanted?"

"It's getting awfully hot in here."

"I don't mind if you turn on the light, D. E. Can you read the paper this way?"

D. E. took a deep breath. He was tending the fire. "Silly," he said. "Awfully silly."

"Do you suppose the baby's going to cry again?"

"Awfully silly," he repeated.

"When I close my eyes or look into the fire, I can still hear the baby crying next door."

Supper was being served in the restaurant downstairs. There was music playing. "You belong to my heart," a trio was singing.

"I know that from Hagibor," Dita said. " 'From the distance lost I'll return . . .' "

D. E. began to whistle along with the trumpet and the saxophone, and Dita sang in Czech the words of the song they were singing downstairs in English: " 'You belong to my heart, now and forever.' "

The restaurant had big picnic tables and wooden chairs. When the musicians took a break, D. E. whistled, "You are my sunshine, my only sunshine. You make me happy when skies are gray."

"Thank you, sir," Dita said in English.

"Not at all."

D. E.'s eyes were gently questioning. His forehead creased. It was a friendly question rather than worry, she thought. He split one of the old shingles and threw it into the fire.

She stretched out on the bed, lying on her side so she could see D. E. "They say everything looks good on me. After all, I don't want to jump off the ship either until it starts to burn or sink."

But she was thinking how she'd come here because she'd wanted to, that she'd done what she'd done all by herself. Her eyes wandered around the room.

"Are you trying to learn everything in the room by heart?" D. E. asked her. They were playing "Dinah" downstairs. And then "Love Doesn't Come Every Day."

"It can never be any lovelier than it is right now, even when all I can do is remember it," she said. She looked around her as if she'd just crossed the Alps or reached the North Pole. "When we experience something marvelous, why do we always wonder how it'll be a year from now or how we'll remember it in fifty years? People are terribly sentimental. Everybody carries around his own private little souvenir album."

"Moonlight Serenade" floated up from downstairs.

"Your memory's like a house with only one person living in it. For one person a whole house is too much."

"Do I have a nice body?"

"How do you mean?"

"Just what I said, David."

"Of course you do!" He didn't hesitate.

"All of it?"

"Absolutely all of it."

"I'm glad to hear you say that."

"Did you expect me to say something else?"

"Nobody ever told me before."

"Well, I'm telling you, right here and now."

"Sometimes I'm not very sure of myself."

"Do you really want me to believe that?"

"I wish you would, D. E."

"Well, you can be sure of yourself from now on."

"In every way?"

"In every way," he replied immediately. "In every way that's important—one thousand percent."

"Everything's different than the way they say it is."

D. E. laughed.

"Have you always been sure of yourself?"

"Boys worry about different things. Nobody usually tells a boy she likes him just because of his body."

"Girls hear that all the time."

"It's certainly true that a girl's body is beautiful."

"Boys' and men's bodies are beautiful too, D. E."

"A boy worries more about being ready, about being able to last, or sometimes about his size. He worries about not being able to make it. He feels guilty and sad and angry. With a boy, you can see it all right away."

She was thinking how she'd probably achieve some of the things she yearned for, but only later. And in a different way. She knew how close she was to teasing, if not exactly offending, D. E. She had no reason for it. He'd only answered what she had asked him.

"Are you scared of something?" D. E. asked slowly.

"Sometimes," she replied, just as slowly. "Whenever I meet someone at night, I think he's a thief. It probably can't be explained—or maybe I just don't want to try. You don't need to worry."

He didn't ask her about what, so that she wouldn't have to explain.

She got up and went over to the window and wrapped the curtains around herself. D. E. went into the bathroom. Where did a girl rank alongside that strong ambition D. E. was trying to tame inside himself?

"The loveliest place in the world," she said through the open door of the bathroom. "It's probably different for everybody, David. In Theresienstadt I looked after children. I think about that more now than I ever did before. Nobody ever wondered

what was going to happen tomorrow or what happened yesterday. 'Now' was all there was. Now is only 'now' too, but nobody
believes it. It may even be richer than before, but there's something missing. Like when the old rabbis say a low wall that's
standing is better than a high one that's crumbling. The thing
that's 'now' ought to be the loveliest thing of all, D. E. There's
only one of every 'now,' isn't there?"

Downstairs they were playing "Begin the Beguine." The music
seemed to come from far away. But it didn't always seem so
distant. The best days and evenings and parties and records
were full of this distance, and it had names, echoes, many resem-
blances. The music brought something distant and close at the
same time, bringing or taking more than was expressed in the
words and the melodies. One world and thousands of different
worlds.

The furniture in the room was old. The paint was peeling
off the mirror's frame. Dita was thinking about her "now" as
if it were a ripe apple ready to eat—though a wormy one. The
pollen on the legs of all the bees that had rubbed against it
when it was still a blossom.

"The way it is now ought to be the best there is, David. I
don't say I'm always like this. But I'm glad you brought me
here. Honest. And that you told me I have a nice body. And
that you didn't even stop and think about it."

She paused. "Maybe fifty years from now I'll like to think
back to this evening and how the baby was crying next door."
She let the curtains slip through her fingers.

"You're like a will-o'-the-wisp. There's more to you than I
can grasp at once."

"You shouldn't repeat yourself, David. I don't want to lose
anything or spoil it."

He looked around the room as Dita had done before. It had
the smell and soul of a hotel room. The head of the bed was
high and carved with curly ornaments—two serpents' heads sur-
mounted by a dove in strange fraternity.

"Fat Munk told me once about what he calls his 'conscious

goal,' " said Dita. "He discovers things the way an astronomer discovers new stars. I'm simply happy, David. You can think whatever you like. I've got to hold my breath, because I can hardly believe it myself. I've been yearning for just a few hours like this. Making a virtue out of necessity. Sometimes."

"What are your plans, so far?"

"To finish this one-year course in the School of Applied Arts, then to study English and French for a year, and later to travel a lot. And you?"

"To finish law school first of all. In the meantime, to make some more contacts with the top people in the I.B.W., and then to jump over their heads to the top contacts in the World Congress."

"Have you heard of those notorious, miraculous Jewish boys?"

"I've only heard of the miraculous rabbis, but I don't believe in them. Look, neither the boys nor the rabbis are with us any longer. Why not grab whatever chances still exist?"

"I'm glad you are honest with me," she said.

Fig leaves carved into the wood repeated themselves across the curve of the bedstead. A chaise longue stood beside the window. Dita's grandmother had had one like it. She spread out the towel and sat down.

"You've got a nice back," D. E. said.

"My God," she answered "everybody's eighteen once, after all!"

She didn't tell him that whenever Doris Lewittova bragged about what she got for it, dinner always ranked last.

"Just because she let Lebovitch sleep with her, Linda pinched the margarine carton he kept his clothes in," she said instead.

"If you're hungry, you can tell me some other way," said D. E. His stepsister had no part in his life, and he didn't want to be reminded of her.

"As glad as I am to be in this world," said Dita suddenly, with her misty smile, "I'd finish it off for myself under certain circumstances faster than anybody can imagine."

Now she knew exactly why she'd come, what she wanted to

do and why, and what a surprise it would be. She felt too that strange kind of tension a person feels when she knows she'll achieve the peace of mind that is perhaps unattainable for some people.

"There are still things I'm ashamed of, which I don't want and never will," she said.

D. E. knew exactly what was going on. Dita was angry for the first time since they'd been here in the hotel.

"When that happened to Liza with the baldheaded doctor who was filling in for Fitz, she started not to give a damn," Dita added.

It took D. E. a second to find the connection.

But she thought she understood why Liza was hanging on to Mr. Gotlob. Liza was very good at pretending. The only ones who were allowed to believe such things were those who hadn't experienced "it" yet. Was that why some Jewish girls only wanted to go with somebody who'd never been there or, in her case or in Tonitchka's case, just the opposite? Is it possible to compare that with rape? The best part of it, she thought, isn't that it can happen to everybody. And the worst isn't that there's nothing good about it. People finally reconcile themselves to other things too.

D. E. gazed at her. There was an expression in her eyes which invited him to come closer and at the same time kept him at arm's length, or perhaps she held herself away from him. Yes or no? He tried to find the reason for the change that had come over her, like watching a stream with many layers to it.

It was only later—and it didn't happen here—that he was able to put it together from what he had known before, including the way she'd been that evening.

But at that moment when she looked up at him, at the wall, at the furniture, and through the window at the stars in a moment of silence, he had the feeling she was looking through him at herself in the mirror. It was a mirror in which she saw something else besides her face, her body, her legs and arms and himself, so close to her.

"I wish I were a grown-up woman," Dita said, "but at the same time, I'd like to be a child so somebody would take care of me, the way I took care of children in Theresienstadt."

"You're not asking for much," D. E. said. It sounded as if he meant the opposite.

"I've never gotten that yet from anybody."

D. E. said nothing. It occurred to him that she lacked that extra quality that would have transformed strong affection into a passion in which a person forgets himself entirely.

"It would revolt me to be like a leech, sticking on to someone else," Dita said slowly.

D. E. got dressed. Dita watched him. He adjusted his tie, his cuffs, his belt buckle. She turned her face toward the warmth of the stove. D. E. looked at her questioningly. She felt like one of Isabela Goldblatova's cats again. Now she wouldn't be able to say that Isabela would put her hand in the fire for her.

"It looks like Brita's going back to England," Dita went on when D. E. kept silent. Probably he hadn't had enough experience yet to give her all the answers. "She'll polish her squire's riding boots in the evening and ask him how his thoroughbreds are getting along," Dita added.

D. E. was drowsy.

"According to Aunt Bella's dream book, lilacs meant a rich bridegroom, a happy love match, and three successful children," Dita said. "Roses also meant love, the dream book said. And love, Aunt Bella's book went on, is like a rose which blooms and wilts, but no one can ever deny that even a wilted rose was once beautiful.

"Guilt and desire at the same time," she went on. "I'm glad you're the one who did it." She felt almost shameless saying it. There was something about him—about his expression, maybe, as he was dressing—that made her say it. You can only get from others what you're able to give, she thought to herself.

"I think I'll go on ahead and order supper," D. E. suggested.

He was showing diplomatic talent. He probably understood

only half of what was going on in Dita's head. And now he gave up.

10

In the garden restaurant, D. E. chose a corner table under a big chestnut tree. His contented maleness was very obvious. When Dita came, he rose and held her chair for her. She was in her dark dress, the top tied at the neck and midriff, the skirt softly gathered and wrapped at the waist.

"That didn't take you so long," he said, exactly the opposite of what she'd expected him to say.

The waiter was quiet and gray-eyed. D. E. kept him hurrying, but the man didn't seem to mind, as if his mind were a million miles away. He brought the menu and waited. Then he took their order and went over to another corner of the garden where a girl sat wearing a black sweater and a locket watch. She was about nineteen, and she sat there with her feet together and her hands folded neatly in her lap. When she looked at the waiter, a smile played across her lips.

Dita could feel herself blushing. She realized that the baby who'd been crying upstairs belonged to the girl and the waiter. Maybe they'd been lying in the same kind of double bed with carved serpents and doves. And there was a child's crib beside the chaise longue, and something had happened that had brought this smile to the girl's lips like a sort of happy echo.

After a while the waiter went into the kitchen and the girl got up and entered the hotel, moving slowly between the tables. There was something very tranquil about her, and she was beautiful in a way Dita couldn't describe in words, because she had only her imagination to go by. She felt her heart beating.

When the girl came back, she was carrying a baby, its hair freshly combed and shiny. She smiled at the waiter as he bent to kiss the child.

Dita looked up at the trees and at the shiny musical instruments. She stroked D. E.'s hand. She looked at the trees and fields and woods beyond the garden and listened to their murmur. The earth was soft and fragrant, and furrowed fields looked like waves of clay.

"This, what is now, ought to be the best there is in life, David," she said. "Maybe I'm an evil person. Sometimes I steal and tell lies, to myself and to you. I cheat—myself and you. But there's not a speck of a lie about the way I feel now. Word of honor."

"I'm hungry as a wolf," D. E. replied.

The waiter brought dishes and silver and salad, and finally a bottle of the red Melnik wine. He wrapped the bottle up to its neck in a white damask napkin. Then he uncorked it and poured, first for D. E., then for Dita, and wished them a pleasant evening.

D. E. raised his glass. He took a sip of wine and began to eat. Dita slowly raised her glass, then put it down again. D. E. had made up his mind not to let things get too serious from now on. Later he paid the bill with the self-assurance of someone who'd been to France and Belgium and Switzerland. She was glad that the tip he left with the change on the saucer was a big one.

The road was narrow, and D. E. drove carefully. Soft night voices filled the darkness. She listened to the sound of the motor, cats meowing, bird cries, horses whinnying. In the distance cars honked and voices were audible.

She wrapped D. E.'s scarf around her neck.

"Some Frenchman said that loving means understanding," she said at last. She said the one word that D. E. hadn't said. "Munk once told me why he thinks the word 'we' is better than 'I.' According to him, all the 'I's are included in 'we.'"

D. E. was wearing goggles and looked like the Italian race car driver Caraciolla.

"Are they really?" he asked.

"This car runs nicely, considering it's such a piece of German junk," she said. She asked him if he was glad he had his own car. D. E. didn't answer. Then she didn't try to tease him anymore.

"I'd like to do something for you, if you'd just tell me what you'd like," he said after a while.

She heard a slightly veiled masculine boast in his words. She could no longer ask him whether it would be fair for her to pay her share for the room and supper, or at least to chip in for the gas. But aside from not saying what she wanted him to say, D. E. hadn't given her any reason to attack him.

They turned into Lublania Street. He stopped a block away from Number 53.

"Thanks, Dita. I don't know about you, but for me it was lovely."

"That sounds like one of those little Japanese poems."

He climbed over the door, went around to the other side of the car, lifted Dita out, and set her down on the sidewalk. The sidewalk was paved with blue and white stones, not very smooth. She gave him back his scarf. They said good night. "You belong to my heart . . ." It suddenly occurred to him that she hadn't behaved like either a virgin or a whore. ". . . now and for ever."

As he drove away, he was whistling, "And the melody under the bamboo tree, my dream . . ."

three

*When I stop on the street to watch children playing and move
a little closer, the mothers look at me suspiciously.*
—GIRL FROM 53 LUBLANIA STREET HOSTEL

Who wanted it that way? Who expected it that way?
—FROM A LETTER BY A GIRL FROM 53 LUBLANIA STREET HOSTEL

1

Every Saturday afternoon Dr. Emil Fitz examined the girls of
Lublania Street. His growing paunch showed under his immaculate blue poplin shirt.

The last sun of the afternoon was falling through the windows.
From the floor below came the sounds of a polka and the voices
of Lev and Isabela Goldblat. Dr. Fitz had taken off his jacket,
and his trousers kept slipping down. He had the chain-smoker's
chronic cough, and seemed on the verge of choking whenever
he was without a cigar.

Linda Huppertova stood half naked before him, clutching her
discarded clothes in her hands as if she couldn't bear to be
parted from them. She stuck out her puny chest for him to
sound, and tried to avoid meeting the owllike gaze he fixed
upon her through his spectacles.

"You should eat and sleep as much as possible, and go in
for sports," he told Linda. "All three at the same time if you
can manage it."

Linda's protuberant eyes had an offended look.

"All right, you can put your things on again. It's just as they say—things move ahead until they return to where they were in the beginning. Next, please!"

Tonitchka Blauova undressed slowly.

"Well, this is like peering into a sardine tin," he said, tapping on her meager body. He spared one glance for Linda Huppertova as she dressed. Having pulled on her sweater, she carefully hitched it up across her bust, to give herself at least the appearance of breasts. It was an old trick of the seamstress trade.

"Child, you're just like a bird," Dr. Fitz said to Tonitchka. "But quite a pretty one at that. Let's say a finch or a starling." He was seized with a fit of coughing that threatened to shake him apart. "There's something inside me, only nobody knows what it is." He sneezed from behind his hands. "If I'm not careful, I see I shall end up like that other doctor."

Linda smothered a giggle with her hand, and Tonitchka blushed scarlet all over. He drew a deep contented breath and patted Tonitchka's thin bottom.

"All right, veil yourselves, ladies, and Miss Saxova can get ready."

"Is there anything the matter with me, Doctor?" asked Tonitchka.

"Too thin, that's all," muttered Dr. Fitz, and lit a cigar. "But we'll make a regular Rita Hayworth out of you before the year's out. I shall be envying your figure myself before we're done."

She gave him a grateful smile for that, even bent her knees slightly as she withdrew, as if dropping him a curtsy. Sometimes she felt ashamed of her body. It was as if she carried within her all the men who raped her, the places, times, and all the circumstances.

"Honestly, you are an idiot, Toni!" said Linda, half in contempt, but half protectively too.

Dr. Fitz and Dita were left alone. At home Dita usually wore a sweater and skirt. By now she already owned three sweaters— a white one, a blue one, and a red.

"You've got quite a nice back, blondie," Dr. Fitz said. "Well, I suppose you're as fit as ever? A man feels almost ashamed to be peeping at you nowadays. What do you intend to do with that beautiful tall body of yours, woman?"

They all knew his erotic theory about the three circles. The first circle included women all over the world, as long as they weren't sick or hunchbacked or something of the sort. The second circle took in the wives of his acquaintances. In the third circle were the wives and daughters of his closest friends. He wouldn't go out with them even if they wanted to. He could go to bed with all the other women without prejudice and keep his self-respect. After old Fatty, he was the most popular old man in the house.

"I'd like to go on that excursion to Switzerland the I.B.W. is organizing," Dita said. "They're looking for people to take care of the children on the way."

"Why don't you make some children of your own?" he asked suddenly. But he didn't give her time to think it over. "How's school going? What are you learning about now?"

"About the architecture of ancient Babylon," she said after a second. "Brown towers made of wood and terra-cotta."

"Don't breathe . . ."

He pressed his stethoscope to her chest. She realized that his reference to school had not been entirely innocent.

"Well," he said. "That's probably what you're really learning. I still remember how amazed I was at how they transported all those stones when the workers had only their hands, muscles, and legs instead of machines. Those beautiful statues really represent the working class of those days, as I am sure our good old Munk would tell us. Yesterday he worried about you. He explained to me the scientific reasons for your frivolity. Of course, he worries about everybody, doesn't he? According to him, frivolity has been very important for a young lady like you. What else has made it possible for you to survive even in the toughest times and overcome obstacles that would have destroyed anybody else under normal circumstances? The circumstances are over, the frivolity has remained."

Dita didn't answer. He liked that kind of talking. He took her pulse and listened to her heart and lungs.

"Much care is being taken, obviously, in the examination of bodies," Dita said.

"We have lived through hard times; we have seen things go from bad to better, and perhaps we begin to believe that there can always be something better."

"A long time ago now, when I asked you if you trusted people, you replied that you did, but only in the daytime, that at night everyone you met seemed to be a murderer."

It sounded like a joke. The room looked very shabby. The house was aging.

Suddenly the doctor turned to her as if he wanted to tell her a joke or confide to her some secret, as a one-time gentleman. "My colleague told me about a beautiful girl who was in an auto accident. They hit a tree and the windshield broke and cut her face so you couldn't recognize her. But that doctor fixed her up so she was even prettier than before. Except she didn't believe it. Her face wasn't what he'd made it but what she saw herself. Men kept paying her compliments, but she took it as if they were rejecting her. She felt they were admiring her mask and not *her*."

He relit his cigar, raising his eyebrows slightly. "Aren't you, by any chance, thinking of emigrating too? Jewish girls make an ideology out of everything."

"Even though sometimes an ideology makes Jews out of everybody else," Dita responded.

"Especially if they're running away from something," he said. "Who promised us that all that's necessary is to invent a lightbulb and there will be no darkness anymore?" he said.

She felt his eyes on her body and on her face, like a touch or a question.

"You are becoming a woman now," the doctor said ambiguously. "Lady luck is being very chummy. I hope you are not easily scared. At least I've never seen anything resembling fear in you."

"I'm scared of sharks," Dita said, smiling. "I dream about them. And the ocean probably has nothing to do with it. It's no use telling Herbert Lagus that I've given up all dreams of future fun in the ocean surf at El Salvador."

"Do you like cold melon?"

"Sometimes," she replied.

"Even in the winter?"

Somebody was yelling in the bathroom at Lublania Street. Dita recognized Linda's voice, then Liza's.

"Don't you dare touch me, you cheap little whore!" Linda shouted. "She's got cancer in her left breast! They opened her up five times! Ask Dr. Fitz if you don't believe me!"

Dita got out of the bathtub and opened the door of the cubicle. She held her towel with one hand and slapped Linda's face with the other. Linda stood confronting Dita, who had goose flesh all over. She was dripping wet.

Even if she'd been stone deaf, Isabela must have overheard, standing in the hall outside the bathroom with her hand on the knob, nodding her long equine head, her big brown eyes glistening.

"Now, girls, what's going on here?" Isabela asked.

"Andy? He's having an affair. He's going with a married woman," Liza said.

Brita started speaking as casually as possible about the most reliable test of skill in the art of kissing. "You take a cherry with a stem into your mouth, eat the cherry, and with your tongue you tie the stem into a knot. If you can do it, you can give yourself the title Woman, with a capital W."

Nobody said a word. In the silence even the motor of the water system below them seemed to grow inaudible.

Lev Goldblat's voice came up through the phenomenal stillness: "Bella, where've you gone? Will someone kindly tell me?

Do you want to drive a man crazy? Which shoes am I to wear with that black suit for the party?"

Isabela, thinner than even a week ago, glanced from face to face and slowly raised her great head. It was as if she had shrunk in front of their eyes.

There was a brief pause while she regained her breath. Then, as though nothing at all had happened, she shouted down gruffly to her husband, "The black ones, Lev." And in the most normal of tones, she said to Dita, "Go on, dry yourself. Do you want to catch cold, you silly goose?"

2

The first spring dance was organized by the management of the Lublania and Krakovska Street homes at the S.I.A. Academic Cafe on Parizska Avenue. Usually it started at eight P.M. At eight-thirty Fitzi Neugeborn was walking toward the bar from the best table, where several of the Jewish Community leaders were already seated.

There had even been a rumor that afternoon in the hostel that Mr. Jacob Steinman, the "former ambassador and great friend of the younger generation," was to be present. This rumor went around before every social event—it had been just the same in February—yet Mr. Steinman hardly ever put in an appearance. It was always said afterward that he'd had a toothache or an attack of rheumatism—always on a scale beyond that of common mortals. A few folks from the International Blue and White Student Union, as well as the ORT persons in charge of the young people's industrial training program, were also there.

"Balzac warned against ladies in violet," the checkroom woman was saying to Dita about Holy Virgin.

Holoubek, the barman, was chatting with Mr. Maximilian Gotlob as if they were still in the middle of the English Channel, retreating from Dunkirk.

"I left my whole platoon behind," Mr. Gotlob announced.

"I've got the same nasty memories of that stretch of beach. I'd rather not think about it unless I absolutely have to," the barman said.

"Bravery and cowardice?" Mr. Gotlob added loudly, so that everybody could hear. "Who knows anything about that? When? Before? Afterward? A year from now?" And he smiled shortly. "Ask me again when I've got more time. An hour after the ambulance squads finish up, a battlefield looks like it's just been plowed. When the deck's burning under a man's feet, he doesn't even have time to notice."

Fitzi Neugeborn gazed at Dita, and Linda watched Fitzi. Andy was tying his shoelace in front of the checkroom. Fitzi was remembering how they used to sing "Boys from Zborov" in two-part harmony back in grade school, and how the teacher had been so touched he'd wept. Fitzi still didn't know where Zborov was. Someplace in the Polish Ukraine? He felt there were too many devices in their talk now instead of real communication. Ambiguous language instead of answers.

It wasn't the meaning of the words he minded. What he minded was the way they were bandied back and forth to the jingling of glasses; yet at the same time he found something attractive in it. It was a sort of skillful and adroit swaggering in front of death, now that they were safe and warm.

"Don't you have anything better to drink than this?" demanded Mr. Gotlob.

"For you, we can always find something, Doctor."

"Did you read about that case in Varnsdorf?" asked Mr. Gotlob. "How can they accuse someone who was in England during the war of Germanizing and then nationalize his factory? I won't even speak of the lack of respect for those who bled for this country when people here were grumbling about weaker beer."

Fitzi was watching them, and the band setting up, and thinking of everything they'd gone through just so these two men could stand here now drinking and calling each other "Sergeant" and "Captain." Perhaps he hadn't had to tremble for his life as they had. Beyond the French coast had always been the coast of Britain, and beyond that the coast of both Americas. Beyond the chimneys of Birkenau there was nothing but, again, only the chimneys at Birkenau. The musicians got nice applause. He saw Dita's hands clapping. The waiters had to bring more chairs for the newcomers.

The band always played three numbers in a row and then took a short break.

Dita's new dress was the color of champagne. She glowed. "Tonitchka, you are the prettiest one here," she said all at once.

"You're very kindhearted," Mr. Gotlob reminded Liza when she offered wine from her glass to Tonitchka.

Tonitchka still looked like someone whose world had been shattered by men, and thus didn't trust them. Or like someone who wanted the one thing she could never have, and wanted things the way they were before it was all ruined.

It was the fascination she felt for people, and at the same time the fear she had of them. She felt a gap between her expectation of what is undeniably good in man and, at the same time, what she knew one man is capable of doing to another. That was why she looked at everybody so closely, with interest and hope, waiting for sparks to jump the way they sometimes do between people. Yet always there was a horror somewhere in the back of her mind of the fact that in every second person, if not in every single one, there lurked a murder, a theft, an act of cruelty.

But she was never quite sure that it was exactly the way she saw it, that what she saw as being the truth might not actually be more than the truth. In reality she suffered from a conflict between a yearning to remember that was just as strong as a yearning to forget.

Dita and Herbert Lagus were dancing by. Dita danced with almost all the boys from 24 Krakovska, going from arm to arm.

"How many times will you steal the essence of a woman's soul?" she said a little later to D. E. as they waltzed by the band.

"Are you only good at the beginning or can you make the long haul?"

The band played the slow end of the melody.

"Thank you," D. E. said.

"With you, every dance is beautiful, like strawberries." Dita told him, smiling. D. E. took her to the bar.

"Can I talk to you a minute, Fitzi?" Linda asked Neugeborn. Never able to express herself as she would have liked, she managed to sound shy and bossy at the same time.

"We can play a hand of pinochle, if you want," Fitzi mumbled.

Linda murmured, "You shouldn't trust somebody who doesn't deserve it, Fitzi. Everybody knows that. It's only you who's blind and deaf." She made a remark about Dita having gotten her dress from God knows where. "Like her jewelry—that bracelet and everything else."

"I don't know what you're talking about."

"She's running around with my brother now."

"What do you want?" Neugeborn's forehead wrinkled. He sighed as though he had been deeply offended. "You're treating me like I'm a privy councilor or something." He tried to smile at her encouragingly. "What's wrong with your voice? You're croaking like a sick raven."

"She really never gave people a fair chance." Linda said. "She looked like someone who would like to feel that somewhere, someplace, there was something, someone, who could make her life happier than it was."

Linda gazed into his eyes and blinked, as if tears were not far away. "I'm not mixing you up with anyone, Fitzi. If you're not interested, I suppose it's your funeral." She smoothed her dress with an offended air, but she didn't move away. She looked toward the bar, in Dita's direction.

"She really believes that by giving five children a few nights' sleep, by telling them fairy tales, she might have saved their lives?"

Fitzi still didn't respond.

"If you are up too high, there is only one way to go—down," Linda concluded.

Fitzi closed his eyes.

Next to them someone was saying that originally, millions of years ago, horses were as small as foxes, that they lived in swamps and had tiny hoofs.

Linda's excitement made the veins swell and throb in her forehead and in her thin throat. She sat rigidly, her fist clenched, her eyes protruding. Yet none of this plainly meant yes or no, and Alfred Neugeborn wanted and needed everything that touched his life to be open and clear. So he said roughly, "Why don't you say right out what you mean? What're you talking about?"

"About the cash box in the Social Welfare Committee's office in Maislova Street that you've fallen in love with," Linda blurted out.

"Nobody's even mentioned it to me," Fitzi said harshly.

"To everybody she says she could have anything she wants, but she is not willing to lift her little finger for it. All she does is smile and hint she has it all in her pocket," Linda went on. "The only thing she ever did for anybody else except herself was in Auschwitz. She took off her skirt and put it under a woman who had a kidney infection. It was very cold then and the woman had been complaining all night that she couldn't lie there on the cold, wet cement floor."

"Couldn't you be good enough to find some enjoyment at least once that wouldn't be at the expense of other people?" Fitzi asked angrily.

"I just don't want you to rush into anything or to expect somebody'll bring soup to you in jail, Fitzi," Linda answered. In her agitation she grasped his thigh. Suddenly she broke into tears. The band played an old wartime hit, "Don't Sit Under the Apple Tree."

Lebovitch came over. He could see what was going on. He spoke coaxingly to Linda. "Don't you think you're making too much noise for the price of one ticket?" He grinned at her.

"Look, little turtle, if you've lost something out of your purse because you're drunk—and you keep losing things, like I lost those pants of mine with you—and if you want to make a scene about it, you've got a microphone right there in front of the bandleader's beefy face. Tell them that whatever honest soul finds it can turn it in at the checkroom for a reward of ten percent of its retail value."

Linda should have known that she was broadcasting information about a crime that had never actually been committed.

"Never get between the bar and a thirsty man," counseled Mr. Holoubek. "If you have the impression the bar's rocking, just kindly stay seated on your bar stools!"

"Excuse me," D. E. said to Dita and got down from the tall bar stool.

He seemed to be heading for the toilet, but he stopped in front of Andy and Neugeborn. "We're not the only people here, you know," he said. "Can't you keep it down?"

Lebovitch knew what was coming. Not a bad stage for a nice fight, he thought. The band had just finished playing "Besame Mucho."

Neugeborn got up, stared at D. E., and then drove his fist against his mouth. Andy began to whistle the "International." D. E., in his English-tailored three-piece suit, took a few more blows and then began to give some back.

Through it all, Fitzi Neugeborn thought of Dita, of everything she'd told him that Friday when he'd visited her, and of everything he'd told her. He supposed he'd made a thundering fool of himself. All that afternoon he'd been preparing for this evening's meeting with her. If he wanted to, he could hate Dita now, and if he hated her enough he would be able to rid himself of his nocturnal visions. It was as if everybody had spat on him. But his fist wasn't as tender or as disappointed as his mind.

For a little while time seemed to stand still. D. E. wiped the blood from his lips, and struck out at Fitzi. There was a sharp crack, like the snapping of two dry twigs, when D. E.'s fist landed.

Neugeborn's right hand was smacked aside and struck Linda in the chest. She let out a wail and clung to her stepbrother.

"Sorry," gasped Fitzi, reeling as if he were drunk. He passed a hand over his breast pocket. The rulers he had taken from the Religious Community store were tucked away like a breastplate.

It was Lev Goldblat who pulled the boys apart, reminding them that this wasn't Chicago, then adding his usual "for better for worse." He stepped in just as Dr. Fitz arrived with the evening's performers, a man and woman billed as "Bronze Statue—Immobile Beauty."

"I'll settle my account later," Mr. Gotlob said as he moved toward the wardrobe.

"Of course," the barman said. *"Buona pacta, buoni amici."*

At a sign from Mr. Traxler, the custodian from 24 Krakovska Street, the band began to play again. The beefy-faced vocalist began to sing in English: "One night when the moon was so mellow, Rosita met young Manuelo. . . ."

There was applause and laughter. Andy led Fitzi Neugeborn out to the checkroom. "We'd better get out of here," he said.

Both boys got their coats. Five minutes later Lebovitch watched uncomprehendingly while the brooding Neugeborn threw the rulers into the gray ripples of the Vltava. It was too dark to see the name on the rulers. Neugeborn tossed in a bunch of pencils too, which floated after them like torpedoes moving toward a fleet of cruisers.

"Some girls want the whole damn world to love them simply because two or three years ago the world almost ate them up with hate," Lebovitch said in his lazy voice.

Neugeborn looked dejected. For him this evening was like an invisible dot at the end of a sentence. He knew there were some noes that could never be said out loud, yet they applied.

Lebovitch put his hand on Fitzi's shoulder. "What do you say, let's go over to the Rumania Bar!" He sounded hearty. "If you want to, Fitzi, I'll lend you my forty-year-old blonde for a few days." He didn't expect Neugeborn to answer.

As the city breathed, it left a glow of many colors in the sky. Higher up, the stars shone white and blue. There was a gentleness at night. The moon was bathing in the river. The empty boats were pitching on the water. Prague was always a peaceful and neat city.

The S.I.A. Academic Cafe was just around the corner from the Rumania. Music filtered out through the ventilators and the open doors. Trumpets, trombones, drums thumping triumphantly. They could hear the beefy-faced vocalist, and the words of his song sounded fuzzy and happy as they slid into the throbbing crescendo of the drums.

3

Isabela Goldblatova, nee Steinitzova, died right after the party.

They all went to the cemetery straight from the meeting with the young men who were recruiting for the Promised Land (capital P, capital L). Brita asked Dita why she hadn't started something with the black-haired good-looking one.

"Maybe I'm just not developed enough yet," Dita replied. "Besides, he's already got forty people, and I've got to look after things here. A leaf is wilted on my rubber plant—although another one has just sprouted."

It had rained through the night, and they felt good that the weather had cleared for the funeral.

"As if you didn't know that with girls it's the other way around," said Liza. "The sooner they start, the sooner they finish."

"If I'd been born a Gypsy, maybe I'd have been more passionate," said Dita.

"You do a beautiful job of make-believe, I can swear to that," Liza assured her.

Tonitchka wondered why people put pebbles on tombstones.

"So you can rot in peace and not be eaten up by vultures, worms, and hens even before you fall apart," Liza murmured. Mr. Gotlob had explained it all to her before.

"Mind and body," Dita said. "They're always mixed up. Do you believe that the manna that fell from heaven onto the desert might have been some kind of lichen that was blown over from Arabia?"

A while before, when the young man began to distribute books, she had asked him for an extra copy and on its flyleaf she had written, "To the champion shadow catcher for the Promised Land. For Theodore Herzl, Dita Saxova, Prague, June, 1947." She had been wearing her gala smile, as she always did in a room full of people.

A pleasant breeze was blowing. Where the path narrowed, Dita walked ahead with Tonitchka. It was quiet there. Sunbeams sifted through the branches. For Tonitchka's sake, Dita took smaller steps. Tonitchka's tiny chin was trembling. Little veins stood out on her forehead. Her shoes were too tight, as though she were a Chinese girl crippling her toes to make her feel smaller.

"I take a size five shoe," Tonitchka said.

"Yes?"

"I could play a boy in an amateur theater company," Tonitchka said, and then she went on: "I heard that in America—or was it England?—they feed cats, dogs, and white mice special food in cans."

"Even during the war?"

"Women painted their legs because the factories were making bombs instead of stockings."

"Oh, I can imagine. Those good Jewish darlings of ours who were, are, and always will try hard to get rich by selling herrings, no matter in which direction or how fast the world rotates to its destruction. Not to speak about their remote cousins who are somewhere, in war or in camps, at the end of their breath."

"It's not in my power or yours to change it." Tonitchka was as docile as grass. Perhaps that was why she had survived. In connection with Tonitchka all acts of violence seemed milder somehow.

"Even the trees are dying," Dita said with a blank expression.

"Perhaps they feel it, somehow, too. It has no meaning for me. Who needs meaning in every millimeter of life?"

"I don't know," Tonitchka said.

"I just like to wander through town these days," Dita said. "I suppose it's because we looked forward so much to coming back here, and yet we didn't really believe we ever would. I don't think I could live anywhere else but in Prague. So I'm like Fitzi Neugeborn in one way anyhow. And yet I've got nobody left in this city. Whenever I talk to the others in school, I feel like a foreigner surrounded by well-meaning strangers. They're all so perfectly balanced. They all belong, if you know what I mean. Even though their opinions may differ. That's funny. They accept me as one of them, but they haven't the faintest idea. Last week I got an invitation to supper at the home of one of these young gentlemen in my class. His father's some kind of technician. After the meal we talked about the faulty material they'd been supplied with at the factory, and about how they'd have to take their umbrellas with them on vacation. They were extremely kind, and meant so well. It was warm and clean in their apartment too. And do you know what that young man dreamed about the night after my visit?" she said. "That he had to go to a concentration camp with me. I guess I made him nervous."

Tonitchka avoided answering.

"Don't you go worrying about your chest measurement," Dita said. "I had trouble just because of mine; in those days, it was better to have none at all. In September of forty-four I lived for a time with some Italian girls in a fairly decent prefab. They took some odds and ends and rigged a bra for me that not even the Technical Museum would want to exhibit these days."

Trees and bushes from the neighboring Catholic cemetery hung over the wall. And higher, where there were no walls or borderlines, the trees were all the same, fresh green and strong. For a while they walked in silence. It was really pleasant here.

"I'm a murderer," Dita said suddenly to Tonitchka. "Of feelings. Relationships. Thoughts. I know exactly what I'm doing when I'm not really doing anything. Sometimes a person lies and steals and kills, all within her own mind. Sometimes I pretend so much that you can hardly call it pretending anymore."

"I know it's already happened to you," Tonitchka said.

"I don't want to think badly of Isabela," Dita said. "I don't know what it is that makes me like that. I keep confronting it in one way or another, a sort of perverted echo. For instance, I still don't like blind or sick people, instead of hating only the sickness or the disease itself. There's some sort of devil inside me. Maybe it's because the Germans kept trying to convince us of our Jewish or Slavic inferiority. Maybe now we really are. Because of what they implanted in us and made us believe."

Brita and Liza caught up with them beside the provisional monument to the victims of World Wars I and II. Mr. Gotlob and D. E. were already standing there. They still had some time before the funeral.

" 'Neither anger nor pity nor compassion,' " Dita said.

"What's the matter with you?" D. E. asked.

"Do you think a Jewish girl from Prague could be anything else if she were in some other place?" Dita responded.

Later, each of them threw three spadefuls of earth into the grave, and Dita was ashamed for worrying about her white gloves. "Death is never just," she said quietly. Munk bowed to the grave. He was dressed the same way as he was in winter. His forehead was beaded with sweat.

"Is he going to blow taps or what?" Brita asked.

"Isabela Goldblatova has died," Munk said at last.

"And I thought she was immortal," Dita whispered.

"The mountain brought forth a mouse," Brita murmured. She really didn't care much for old Munk. Probably on behalf of the British Royal family she resented those favorite maxims of his, like "People were born to be equal" or "History will bring about equality, sooner or later."

Munk pulled a sheet of paper from the pocket of his overcoat and spoke about echoes that come from other echoes, about Isabela's three sons—Ignac, Arthur, and Arnost—as if their ashes had blown across fields and nourished flowers—or weeds or wheat or moss.

The skin of Munk's neck quivered like a rooster's comb. It hung in wrinkles from his throat and chin, webbed with bluish veins and tendons, protruding like an old dog's. His skin was the color of parched clay. His eyes were sad. If death were suddenly to appear and tell one of them, "It's your turn now," he would not hesitate a moment to offer himself in their stead. Perhaps he only wished it were nighttime, when everybody would be asleep and he in his bed. He was holding a copy of the *Jewish Gazette* and he read it aloud.

"Permit a few words from a veteran who served in the army abroad. I did not join the army late. My call-up number was 272. I fought in the battle of Sokolovo and in all the other battles until finally reaching Prague with General Svoboda's army. I went from a light machine gun all the way to a Maxim. There were three brothers in my company who were Jewish too. Two of them fell in battle. The youngest, age sixteen, was also at the front. The General himself gave the order that he shouldn't be assigned to the firing line. He wanted to save him for his mother, since her other two boys had fallen. I was wounded, losing a pound of flesh from my right side. I had not fully recovered when I volunteered to return to the front. I did so although I no longer had any chance of defending any of my own people. My parents had been killed, my brothers and my wife were murdered, my child was murdered. I very much regret what is happening today and that people talk as if we had joined the fighting only at the last minute."

This was part of the speech that had been given at the meeting of the Community governing board by ex-Sergeant-Major Julius Schwartz, the warehouse attendant, before he jumped out the window.

"When I was with Grandma Olga at Habry, I used to feel as good as I do now," Dita said. "If I had a little patch of ground, I'd grow something on it."

Andy said, "Julius Schwartz has a headstone just a few graves away from Isabela's. I see we still wink at suicides."

"Would you want to leave him lying out on the street?" asked Brita.

"If somebody wants to kill himself, go ahead," Andy agreed.

"But first I'd certainly want to settle a few accounts."

According to the *Jewish Gazette,* people had died "quietly and unbendingly." Or "quietly, humbly, and patiently."

The smell of roast meat filtered in from the gravedigger's house. It was a chicken, or perhaps a duck or a goose, and its aroma mingled with the smell of sauerkraut.

"From roast lamb to roast people and back again," Liza remarked.

"Aren't you reading the *Jewish Gazette* too much?" Andy asked. "What good does it do you?"

When old Lev Goldblat looked at them he smiled, as if to say that when the body passes away, not everything passes away with it. His half smile surprised nobody.

"I would like to know what is beyond the stars," Tonitchka said.

"We are burying a courageous Jewish mother," Munk was saying. "Her sons were like three trees. She was born to last."

Dita was listening to the leaves rustling and thinking about D. E. and about Munk. Every tree in every grove, and every blade of grass, smelled like honey.

A few minutes later she left the cemetery with Erich Munk. It was a lovely day. The river and the Old City looked friendly, and she could feel how close it all was to her. The voices in the street were speaking in some secret code understandable only to someone who was born here and felt at home.

"Maybe you're growing up too fast," said Munk as they walked through the Old City toward Charles Bridge. He knew that she'd never been to the cemetery before. As far as he knew, neither Fitzi Neugeborn, Andy Lebovitch, nor David Egon Huppert ever went to a cemetery, on principle. Not just because they had no one there. None of their families had a grave.

"Is that good or bad in my case?" asked Dita. The stream moved slowly, and the colors of the water mirrored the blue sky. The river was very clean. She was thinking of the trip to Switzerland.

"How did you like Turgenev?" he asked.

"It's still ringing in my ears. 'Why can't we ever tell the whole truth?'"

"What are you seeing Mr. Gotlob about?"

"Not about any legal matters, fortunately. He'd find out I don't have a very high opinion of lawyers."

"Books aren't your worst friends." Munk kept walking. He said nothing about responsibility or innocence, as he had when he'd talked of the road that leads from insecurity to danger, but told her that, even so, he worried about her.

He was thinking about that immortal hunk of English literary flesh from *The Merchant of Venice* that was in the consciousness of so many in so many countries, east and west of the Elbe. Although it was perhaps only the offspring of a vision inspired by all sorts of things, while this real, bleeding piece of flesh from the body of a soldier in an Eastern army would probably be forgotten just as quickly and properly as the first one would be remembered.

"You're failing in almost all your subjects," he said.

She no longer tried to convince him that she'd been intact for too long, but she couldn't tell him anything outright. Gulls were performing their acrobatic stunts. "One can see disaster coming, but is powerless to court it and save oneself." She'd gotten that from his Turgenev too.

"To know more, see more, and hear more means to *be* more," Munk said.

"I'm happy to be in this world," she said, smiling. "I discovered that all men are prostitutes to one degree or another. It is the way of man. Everything is based on trade, whether moral or immoral. So the question of morality must be kept apart from the question of prostitution."

"But, Dita—"

He couldn't reconcile himself—in spite of all that had happened—with the claim that all values were relative, that there was no ethical absolute. She told the fat little man about the small ceramic pitchers she'd made last week and how she had broken the ones that hadn't turned out right. She asked him if he'd like to have one, glad she could hint at a different kind of breakage.

He was as nervous as he'd been last week when he'd given her a hundred-crown bank note. She had learned how to accept gifts now; she wondered why there wasn't a picture of wolves on bank notes instead of naked women.

"I heard you have a gold bracelet," he said. "No one seems to know how you got it. But don't tell me unless you want to. Perhaps next time. I'd like to meet you more often."

They walked side by side for a while, an unmatched couple, a misalliance, Dita's hair hanging loose, her bearing erect and graceful. Suddenly they didn't know what to say to each other.

"Never take anything from people you don't know," her mother used to tell her. "And even if someone gives you something, try to pay for it. Don't let anybody give you something for nothing. Nothing is ever for free." She looked at her bracelet. My God, did Munk think that maybe she'd gotten it the way some girls got gifts from mysterious men? Why had he avoided her eyes? Would he want to go out with her? Or she with him? She knew it was a lot of nonsense.

She spoke in her mind all the words that hadn't been uttered aloud. "You've grown up much too fast" was code for "You're depraved!"; and "You're quite shameless!" or "Aren't you too carefree?" was the probable translation of "What will become of you in a year's time?" Or else "The best finally always do what must be done." Of course, everything changes, including words and their meanings; "only numbers stay the same." She felt her days going by like snow under the sun. She knew she was living a rather shabby existence and that she ought to do something about it. She continued watching the gulls. They were white and elegant in flight.

She almost left Munk standing on the bridge while she ran down the steps to Kampa Island.

4

Maximilian Gotlob turned up in front of the I.B.W. library in Mala Karlova Street wearing his black Borsalino. He looked like a British cabinet minister. He smiled like a man who knew what was what. He pressed his lips to her white kid glove. Then he suggested that they have their little talk somewhere between four walls. He recommended the Sophocles bar.

"Well, don't you like pleasant surprises? How well you are looking, my child," he said, smiling with the sophistication of a man who knows what he's talking about.

The manager of the Sophocles night club came forward at once to greet them.

"A table for two, please!" Mr. Gotlob said, a little more emphatically than was necessary. "One must try to take the bad along with the good, my dear. I've been alive long enough to have learned that. Personally, I prefer the evenings to the mornings. Some day I'll explain why."

They were given a table for two next to an elegant pillar inlaid with mirrors all the way up to a tall man's height. The Gypsy orchestra, headed by Mr. Egon Lewit from the Jewish Community, played an old hit.

Mr. Gotlob turned to Dita. "What kind of day have you had? Luckily, the weather's been lovely." He smiled and made himself comfortable. "How do you feel, my child?"

"I've just left that category," she answered.

"Oh, yes, by the way, Liza asked us to excuse her. You probably know why." Mr. Gotlob smiled with all his chins, just like her Uncle Carl. He was trying to give her the impression that tonight the world was theirs, with no graves. She'd never been here before. Ye gods, Dita said to herself, I'm a hopeless ninny. Maybe I am worse than the rest. I don't know. Perhaps we're all only whores after all. Always on the edge. Why? I know why. It's no secret to me. But why the hell do I always have to resurrect phantoms, even if they're only phantoms from the past? She'd been prepared to enjoy herself and to get a little drunk with

Mr. Gotlob. But whose judgment was slipping? Should I spoil things right from the beginning by feeling guilty about Liza Vagnerova, repeating those few Italian code words of hers like *sangue?*

"I hope you're hungry as a wolf, my dear." Mr. Gotlob smiled at her. "Do you know my favorite saying? 'We may permit ourselves everything, as long as nobody catches us!' " He could feel the hunger in her, a kind of greed, a self-centeredness for which only women are forgiven. Or was that only the way he saw it?

For just a moment, right after they sat down, it seemed they wouldn't have anything to say to each other.

"Will you allow me to order? Have you any special preferences or will you trust my judgment?" asked Mr. Gotlob.

She could feel the blood rushing to her face. She thought about liking and disliking her body this week. And about how difficult it was to make someone happy, including herself. The way that Mr. Gotlob had watched her and how the sound of his voice had somehow taken the breath and strength out of her.

"Do you like strawberries?" asked Mr. Gotlob.

As a first course, Mr. Gotlob ordered a spiky-fleshed fish, *à la Grecque.* This was followed by American UNRRA canned turtle soup afloat with delicious fatty bits of turtle meat. Then came veal steaks *à la Holstein* that melted in your mouth, served with golden French fries. The fragrant cheese strudel, fresh from the oven, was nearly as pretty to look at as the bowl of strawberries under snowy whipped cream that followed. The soup made her think of the sea; the strawberries in the pure white cream were blood-red. She was impressed with how very elegant it all was.

"Are you still a supporter of the International Blue and White, Mr. Gotlob?" She felt almost sticky, as if she'd taken a bath in ice cream and then gone out into the sun to dry.

"I support excellence everywhere," said Mr. Gotlob. "In London I could show you at least a dozen places superior to this.

I wish you could see the Four Hundred or the Caprice. I'd have begun with oysters and finished with dessert. Or the other way around—dessert first, oysters at the end."

The wine had a green tint, like the surface of a cold lake. By now she thought only occasionally of her father in his shabby clothes, and how he used to invite her out for lunch and order one and a half portions of something called "grenadier march," which was noodles mixed with potatoes and onions. She drank some more.

"You really like strawberries so much?" asked Mr. Gotlob as she put one into her wine. "Why?"

"Because of the way they go into your mouth," responded Dita. "And then, they taste good." Her face grew rosier and brighter, as from a kind of fever; her eyes were shining as if she'd never known discontent.

"How did you spend the rest of the day?"

"I went for a walk with Mr. Munk."

She was thinking that this was the third time today her dark dress had come in handy.

There was a pause and she could hear how Munk's name must sound to Mr. Gotlob. He raised his eyebrows slightly.

"Does he shout, 'Death to your class!' at you the way he did to me when we were talking about social welfare at the board meeting of the Community?" asked Mr. Maximilian Gotlob.

"We talked about school." She felt guilty not taking old Fatty under her protection.

"He'd be a regular bleeding heart, if anybody'd bother to listen to him. He said we ought to sell the Community's property and give the proceeds to the welfare department. He'd like to heal the whole world. A new edition of Karl Marx, that's Munk."

She looked around. Soft music and champagne, white table-cloths, red lights, and a discreetly attentive waiter. She inhaled deeply. She thought about how it is for Gypsies as it is for Jews. They both look like everybody else in the country where they live, and at the same time they are made to feel so different.

"I can see you're a connoisseur of the arts," said Mr. Gotlob. "There's a tinge of sweetness to it—and a slight acidity," she remarked, looking into her wine glass. She felt that she was being rather nasty. Honey on the tongue and poison in the heart? Mr. Gotlob drank his wine slowly and looked at her with interest.

"We're living on a savage planet, child," he said. "We've bled and died and others are slicing up the victory cake. Everything's been divided, even the family luncheon table."

He took a roll, broke it into two parts, and, holding one part, slowly bit into the other. He said that regarding her conversation with Liza about killing, his idea was that their people didn't kill each other with knives or pistols so much as with business transactions. "Just as cruel as with a knife, God knows," he said.

"It's interesting listening to you." She saw her image in the mirror.

"I've already lived through quite a lot, my child," he said with his mouth half full. "And as someone who's fought, I've got a right to say this: If we got up right now, you and I, and ran forward and missed each other and kept running, we'd have to run around the whole globe before we found each other again. But by the time we did, this place would have changed. It would belong to someone else. The people who treated us like victors two years before, yelling, 'Welcome!' now would say, 'Sorry, ladies and gentlemen—or comrades—this place is occupied. You've come too late.' " Mr. Gotlob waited while the head waiter poured the rest of the wine. "I'd be happy, Dita, if at least the law of the jungle applied here. And not, of course, because I have such an admiration for jungles."

There was a melancholy in the Gypsies' music which you could attribute to anything you wanted. Mr. Gotlob looked strong and complacent.

"They play very nicely," she said. "They really do."

He was smoothly shaven. According to Liza, Mr. Gotlob shaved twice a day. He had a bald head with a heavy bulging forehead. He wore a dark expensive suit with a vest, an immaculate white shirt, and a burgundy tie. He looked like a man of letters.

"You have lovely eyes, my child," he said. "You've got a very sensitive face. You look like a peach."

"It's funny how easily all this melts away a guilty conscience," said Dita.

"My goodness, child, why a guilty conscience? Time heals all. And so does this." He raised his glass.

She was listening to some distant echoes. "Red is the color of hope, my children." Or, "There are always two sides to every slice of bread we eat." Once Munk told her, "I am quite sure that whatever we do for those near to us—or those not so near—we do for ourselves at the same time. The destiny of every man is, to a certain extent, my fate too. And it doesn't matter to what extent I realize this now or later or maybe never. Being aware of the goal is just as important at your age as the goal itself." It was really "very grand and very ridiculous." Why does everyone expect so much—in all possible directions—from something that cannot give him everything?

She saw herself as she was long before her days at 53 Lublania Street: a lean, lanky child sitting on a pavement outside the laundry at 7 Josefovska Street, a tall girl with blue eyes and fair hair, seen as if in the reflection of the sun. And then her mother's contralto calling her in to lunch. A few hops and jumps, as though she were wearing seven-league boots and had to cross mountains and valleys. Amidst the vaporous scent of other people's washing she ate soft dry bread and drank a cupful of watered milk, the best lunch imaginable in the Sax household on weekdays, with the exception of Saturdays, and sometimes even including them.

Father would be there washing his hands. And after a while, before reaching for the towel, he would make his usual remark about how lucky they were that there was still enough work. "A poor man has to work for everything he gets. Mind you, I'm not saying I wouldn't like to be in the money. Not for our sakes anymore, but for yours, Dita." So this is how we invite people who don't exist anymore to our parties, she thought.

112

Enough work meant hampers and boilers full of dirty linen. Later on enough work came to mean shoes that needed mending. But one day maybe their daughter, Dita, with the lovely name that went so well with the color of her eyes and hair and her gentle complexion, would live in a beautiful white house where everything would be pleasant and elegant and clean. Soon her father had had to look up when he spoke to her.

When they'd all been together, because all of them were still alive, the world seemed beautiful to her, even if it was a poor one. It hadn't yet become a contest to see who would be first or who could at least stay in the running.

In the mirrors Dita could see how the blood had flushed her skin. The back of Mr. Gotlob's neck looked like a ruddy furrowed chunk of wood set off by the plum blue of his English suit.

"I wanted to ask your advice about that summer excursion of the International Blue and White to Switzerland, Mr. Gotlob."

"Certainly, my child," he answered slowly, like somebody who expected this question. "After all, someone's got to go, so why shouldn't it be the best and the prettiest? As a matter of fact, we selected you this very afternoon. Mr. Huppert hasn't told you yet? Really, didn't he tell you? You'll go either with a group of children or on a study grant to Grindelwald. We still don't know yet. But we won't make you wait long. You'll be informed as soon as possible." Then he added, "No one should ever make anyone wait too long for something he really wants, don't you agree?"

"Thank you, Mr. Gotlob." She could feel the blood rushing to her face. He went on to say that it was enough just to sit across from her and look at her, congratulating himself on the miracle of her return.

When the Gypsies began to sing—all five voices in chorus— her eyes lit up. "How can I show you my gratitude?" she asked him.

"I wonder what a person could want from such a beautiful girl as you are, child?" Mr. Gotlob coughed.

"I hope I'll be able to arrange that."

"Are you passionate?" Mr. Gotlob smiled.

"It all depends on what you mean by that."

"Laws are there to be gotten around, my child," he said to her suggestively.

She was silent for a while. Then she said, "I guess I'm drunk, Mr. Gotlob."

"Goodness gracious, from those few drops?"

"It's terribly hot in here, Mr. Gotlob. And it's been such a long day."

"We haven't drunk a toast yet to Grindelwald, child!"

"I really thank you very much, Mr. Gotlob. You're really terribly kind."

"Here's to your gentle loveliness, Dita. You're not a child anymore. You've really left that category." He paused, then said with a sigh, "When this wine was made somewhere on the Rhine, Otto Bismarck was still alive. Oh, well, mention Bismarck and you have to think of Hitler next. Is it true that one of the boys from Krakovska Street has bought a dog and is calling it Hitler? Of course, we can change the wine for some champagne."

He leaned closer. She could smell the rankness of his breath. She could feel his hand, his eyes, his breath, like a hot and silent wind, tearing the clothes off her body. She could see herself in the mirror smiling.

"Petit à petit, a chacun son nid," said Mr. Gotlob with a smile.

"What does that mean?"

"Bit by bit, every bird builds his nest. But tell me about yourself, child. Your life interests me. You're too modest. Liza often talks about you. Mr. Huppert has told me about you too. You must be very popular among the people in the I.B.W. I'm glad we've finally found an opportunity to get better acquainted." He raised his glass. "To . . . a closer friendship?"

"As a soldier in the overseas army, you've probably been in worse situations than this," she said. She did look pretty. She was tall, reserved as much as tired after the long day. There was something pure in her face. Suddenly she laughed. She'd drunk too fast and too much. Everything struck her as funny.

"We were plunked into it as young men," said Mr. Gotlob, draining his glass. "You lose your friends from your platoon, and they weren't all rookies either. And even if you manage to stay alive, you just feel guilty, always certain that something's wrong. Luck's never been distributed fairly. It makes no difference that you're not doing badly, that you have a decent job and a nice bank account. When you get up in the morning and ride to your job in the streetcar with all of the other workers, you have certain regrets."

"What did you do in the army, Mr. Gotlob?"

"I was an accountant, my dear. First an accountant, then in a fighting unit, and finally back to my old job."

"I should really be getting back to Lublania Street."

"Here's to your sweet ripe beauty, Dita! And to those who haven't got it anymore."

He touched her glass with his own and peered keenly into her long pretty face as she looked back at him with a slightly bitter smile. Here, he thought, is a generation that is clever and, quite illogically, also carefree. These youngsters were strong and at the same time weak. For them life was no longer a matter of being on the right side or the wrong side, but of surviving or not surviving. They no longer seemed terrified by what they didn't know, but rather by what they knew for sure. They were like a patch of unburned grass in the middle of a blackened field. They were closer to the jungle than they were willing to admit. Was it so? Maybe. At least it was a part of the whole picture.

They had the same goals as his generation, but not the same motivations. They'd encountered something that had destroyed their capacity for extended self-denial. They were modest, but only in the way of those who are strong and therefore, often undemanding. Patience was probably the first rung on their scale of values.

For them no law represented justice. Law was never an issue. It was a stick to beat them with, a rope to hang them with, a poison to kill them with. Their barometer didn't indicate the pressure that is, but the pressure that was. They didn't believe in fifty more years of peace that would balance the past fifty years of wars.

In their own way these youngsters had even become an accusation and a burden that caused misunderstandings in the remnant of the Jewish Community. What they would never attain was predictable, and this alienated them even more, instead of bringing them closer to the Community. Even though they didn't have it inscribed on their foreheads that the rest of the world owed them something, it had, in Mr. Gotlob's opinion, gotten into the marrow of their bones. Their hands were outstretched and their pockets were bottomless. Their sense of gratitude had withered. They had the same kind of arrogance war invalids have. They let themselves be fed by foreign organizations, as if they were accusing those who were running those organizations of not having experienced a fraction of what they'd lived through, so they weren't even obliged to say, "Thank you." They seem to say, "Go live for an hour—a minute, a second— where we spent months and years. If you live through it, we'll ask you candidly how you managed to survive and at what price. Then we'll see how you behave."

They grasped after parties and good times, regardless of what class they belonged to. They snatched up apartments with bathrooms, elbowed their way into schools for which they didn't always have the proper qualifications, signed up for excursions abroad, for things they'd never even dreamed about before.

Their Pied Piper was Munk, and Munk's Pied Piper was the Revolution. According to them, the old world, which had led directly to the slave labor and KZ camps and gas chambers, didn't deserve to survive. And they played their pipes both East and West. But actually, weren't both choices only the excuse for finding a more comfortable chair for their bare rumps, a roof over their heads, and something to put in their bellies? Only then did they ask themselves what it was called, where it came from, and to whom it belonged.

For them the world was like a fruit tree in an autumn orchard, which they hadn't even known about in the spring and which would be barren after the first snowfall. They were more interested in ripe fruit than in orchards and how things grew. What they wanted they wanted *right now*—no time to waste.

They enjoyed freedom. The more they had of it, the more they wanted. And yet, so it seemed to him, freedom was the first thing they were ready to sacrifice. The flood was neither behind nor ahead for them, but in their very blood.

He often objected to their manners. It wasn't just that it never occurred to them to get up from the table until they'd finished everything on their plates. Or that they were never in any hurry (to put it mildly) to answer letters. Or that they treated their belongings as if they'd stolen them or were about to lose them, no matter what they'd cost.

It took three times as much effort for them to understand what was appropriate. Was that because—before—they had learned to treat things in a way that was inappropriate and indecent?

They had their own particular yardstick and rules, but the meaning of words had shifted. They forgave the past for nothing. And there was always somebody around who personified the past for them. They spoke one language and heard another beneath it. They behaved like gamblers who know how much depends on luck and how much on skill. They divided people into a few basic categories and wasted no time on details.

They expected generous treatment because of what they'd gone through, without wanting anybody to identify them with those from whom they wished to collect interest.

In many ways, they appreciated life as nobody before them had. They had come to savor life as a fleeting gift, and to take its only alternative—death—as casually as one of the dishes in a lunch or dinner meal.

A sort of nervousness sometimes made them act friendlier than the friendship they were capable of giving, and sometimes more unfriendly than they really felt.

Sometimes he had an almost perverse yearning to go where

they had been, at least for a day, if only to understand it.

Mr. Gotlob felt a bit guilty and slightly cheated, but he understood. He was ready for the ironies of life. He was old enough to know the rules of the game. He couldn't tell them that what you've gone through can't protect you in the slightest against what still lies ahead. He watched the band, the neighboring tables, the waiters. The more of these girls he was with, the more democratic he felt. Each time one of them got pregnant, she had an abortion. Except for Doris Lewittova—the exception that proved the rule. Until finally they stopped getting pregnant. He could testify that this was a generation that, at least in physical relations, had abandoned all taboos. They were more open, to say the least. The things their mothers and fathers had considered prohibited and perhaps perverse they did with a naturalness that restored their original innocence.

Dita Saxova was certainly one of the prettiest, a ripe young girl with a grown-up smile. But when she asked him to use his influence to help her and when she'd gotten what she wanted, she didn't make any effort at camouflage. She'd been pampered, but in a strange way, upside down, he decided.

Dita noticed the way he was looking at her. She smiled, as if the difference in their ages had moved from his chair to hers.

After another glance at her peachlike skin, Mr. Gotlob returned to his first interest. "I'm really very intrigued by you, Dita. I know that you have been careful, so far, not to let anyone come too close. That you are trying hard to be the sort of a girl who is not easily taken advantage of. But life is always a kind of transaction, isn't it?" He raised his eyebrows slightly. "Tell me, what are you interested in most?"

"In antiques." She waited for Mr. Gotlob to get up and slap her face.

Instead he kissed her hand. "Anything you want, Dita."

"I've had too much to drink. I can't stand this heat."

"You're fresh as grass, child, believe me. I wouldn't steer you wrong."

"I'm drunk, honestly I am. I'm totally drunk."

"Let me tell you something, honey. Nobody can ever take away what we have and enjoy. Unless they take us with it." He chuckled. "Listen, Dita, you're a sensible girl. We can speak on equal terms. After all, I too know about secrets that are binding on both sides, and about pleasures that are only momentary—and not only because of my age. Nothing before, nothing after. That's it. Nothing else. But this is an advantage, nothing after, not a disadvantage."

Dita leaned back against the plush chair. *Sophocles. Sophocles.* The name of the bar was shining above the bandstand. In the mirror she could see what she was displaying for Mr. Gotlob's admiration. Fish, little fish, the smallest fish of all, the road to Switzerland is now open.

Mr. Gotlob's eyes, heavy with wine, feasted on her white neck. Her hips were slim, and her hands made him think of the same thing her legs and her loins did. Then he leaned toward her big blue eyes and her slightly parted lips. "May I invite you to dance, child?"

"I'm drunk, I really am, Mr. Gotlob. I am already one hundred percent drunk."

Holding her elbow, he helped her to her feet. She was embarrassingly taller than he, and she automatically reminded herself not to stand up too straight. Somebody had asked the Gypsies for "Jericho." She felt she had entered the kind of contest a woman could only lose. The Gypsies immediately began "Jericho." All the trumpets were in full swing. And the drums. She felt something stirring in the air and adjusted her white silk scarf. She smoothed her dress. The red velvet, red curtains, and red napkins on white tablecloths seemed to glow. Even things that weren't red seemed rosy to her.

"I can't stand on my feet," she whispered.

"I knew you wouldn't let me down, Dita."

"The whole room is rocking up and down."

Mr. Gotlob led her out onto the dance floor. He beamed complacently. She felt as if she were on a boat. Twinkling fragments of mirror cast points of colored light down on them. The Gypsies seemed to be tireless. They continued playing, singing, and smiling. Their dark faces shone as though covered with oil. They had beautiful teeth. She could feel Mr. Gotlob's right hand brush casually across her breast when they turned. The floor was as shiny as ice. His hands were so hot and his breath was warm on her neck. She tried to draw away, but couldn't prevent him from touching her again. He looked at her closely, at her mouth and neck, her breasts and her hands. The Gypsies were singing, "Jericho, Jericho," while Mr. Gotlob whispered the usual things in her ear. She tried not to breathe for a while.

"You've really matured all over, haven't you?" Maximilian Gotlob said. "If you'd let me, I'd drink you like a ripe peach. To the last drop."

She avoided looking at his face.

"I'd like to tell you what a beautiful figure you've got, if you'd allow me to be quite honest, and if you were wearing nothing else but your bracelet."

The remote echo was suddenly very close. She laughed again, louder than she should have. The lights spun like falling stars. Everything melted in the swimming red glow. Her stomach felt heavy. Then in an instant she was almost sober again, even though her knees felt unstable, like standing on a ship in a strong sea. Nothing was clean. She stopped, afraid she was going to throw up.

"I like you very much, Dita," he said. "I waited as long as I possibly could to meet you alone."

"I think I despise you," she said slowly. "Even though you've been kind enough to arrange the trip for me and I need you."

She left Liza Vagnerova's bridegroom-to-be standing in the middle of the dance floor. The name *Sophocles* flashed once more over the bandstand. She didn't hear him muttering, "Worse than a whore . . ."

5

In the bathroom back at Lublania Street, Dita slipped out of her dress. She felt sticky. She looked at her underpants. Not a drop. Water plunged noisily into the old porcelain tub. Downstairs in what was once the kitchen Liza was looking after Lev Goldblat.

Dita slid into the tub. Her teeth were chattering. She waited impatiently for the feeling of refreshment. The water was like ice. It made her body feel lighter. Nothing like that happened to her mind, though. It was like lead. What game am I playing? she asked herself.

Her eyes burned. The lids were heavy. Something's got to happen, she said to herself. I've got to be punished. She shivered. Who said everything's going to be weighed, everything measured? She couldn't understand herself. What was it that pushed her where she never wanted to go? When she was alone, there was no need to lie to herself, was there?

Out of nowhere, Dita thought of the girl in the black sweater. She wished she could scrap everything and start all over again. Lately this feeling came to her more often. Like an echo, upside down. She submerged herself up to her chin in the cold water. She might do some drawing or some writing . . . maybe stage design? There were things preferable to that. She tried imagining Lev Goldblat's dreams. Some people believe that as long as you're able to dream, you're alive. How right are they, really? Maybe they just go to the movies too often. When you occasionally succeed in forgetting yourself, things don't seem quite so bad. A memory is never entirely true, but it isn't a lie either. One night the custodian told her he had dreamt he was standing in line for selection when they pulled Isabela away from him. Then he was running after one of his sons, and he had almost caught up with him when he woke up. The family was his and Isabela's work. Ignac had been a plumber, Arthur an electrician, and Isabela had wanted Arnost to be a doctor. She was like a tree. Sons were her branches. But some obstacles were invisible, unknown, unpredictable. Either the branch is strong enough to survive or it dies. And a storm was bad. It wasn't her fault, though, Dita said to herself. Many things lost, confused—perhaps. Grace and disgrace. God, what I can't do for myself will never be done.

A door squeaked. Dita looked up, startled, but glad for the company. It was Liza Vagnerova. She cast a knowing glance at Dita's rumpled clothing and her soaking body.

Dita gave her a smile and sighed.

"Are you so rich already?" Liza asked, hanging Dita's things on the rack.

"I seem to be heading that way, thanks, just like you," she said. More and more tension was building up inside her.

"Let me know when you get there."

Dita felt herself blush.

"The girls say that instead of eating meat or chocolates, you sometimes feed yourself with sleeping pills," Liza said.

"Who can get along entirely these days without some kind of pills? On principle I don't overdo it, don't worry. What do you do when you've got a toothache or a headache?"

"Why do you have a headache?"

Dita laughed, using her smile that was good for all occasions.

"You must be sick anyway," Liza said. "Munk was here at least eight times looking for you," she went on. "I hope you're not getting involved with him. He says he's arranged for your make-up exams. All you have to do is fill out the application."

"Thanks. I just don't know what to do for him."

"Why even bother to talk about it?" Liza said.

Dita was silent.

"Considering how you look, you're unbelievably innocent," said Liza.

"I wish I could understand," Dita said, smiling. "I wish I knew exactly what it is I want and when I want it. As it is, all I have is the feeling that I need something." As if some things were windows through which you could look inside. She realized that sometimes she assumed people could tell what she was thinking about.

"A lot of people envy you simply because you're pretty," Liza said. "I'll bet plenty of people try to flatter you. If I were you, I'd believe them as much as last year's snow."

Dita felt like someone who suddenly has the feeling that she's been asleep for a long time and has just awakened.

"What were you talking about with D. E. so long? Do you still have so much to say to each other?" Liza asked.

"About ships and different countries where the International Blue and White goes and how to get among those who are chosen and what you can expect from it all."

"Under what conditions wouldn't you stay here?" Liza burst out. "I've experienced those debates about ships with Mr. Gotlob."

"Did he tell you too about the ones that are unsinkable?"

"For Maximilian Gotlob, there's no such thing as an unsinkable ship."

"Tell him to take you to see the movie about the *Titanic.*"

"I doubt he'd want to see it a second time. He told me how majestic the icebergs look."

"Isn't it absurd that we've survived our parents?" Dita asked all at once.

"Why?"

Dita gazed at the porcelain sides of the bathtub, at the shower head and the wooden mat. "Sometimes the whole world feels like one big concentration camp," she said. "Or a network of camps. You can get transferred from a better one to a worse one or the other way around, but you can never get out."

"You shouldn't blaspheme," said Liza. "Honestly, sometimes you've got a twisted sense of humor."

Dita got out of the bathtub. She looked at the same time like a swan and like a stork. She clutched Liza's skinny shoulder. Liza looked tired. Her bones seemed barely covered by skin, and her skin barely covered by a thin robe. Dita could feel Liza's body and her own wet skin. She threw her arms around Liza's neck.

6

They lay down side by side in number 16.

"Remember when you were going with that old doctor, Liza?

Are you really going to marry Mr. Gotlob?"

Liza leaned on her elbow. "Why do you ask me that? And why right now? What do you think of him?"

"He could play the bald butler in some farce—the one that brings in a letter on a tray and says, 'Your lordship, there's a corpse outside!'"

"I don't look at it with resignation. I've gone with older men and younger ones. It all comes down to the same thing."

"It must be revolting, letting yourself be touched by a big soft belly. I don't mean him." She was wearing blue pajamas with a fringed sash.

"There are worse things than bellies." Liza giggled. "That's why some girls marry older men." She was trying to whisper. "Maybe it already turns my stomach. Any kind of sensuality, even the so-called healthy sort with young boys. That's all anybody cares about. Doesn't it revolt you, the way they all want it? There's never any joy to it. Unless I can say, 'Yes, yes, this is what I really want.' Ever since spring I've been glad just to get it over with. I've learned how to pretend satisfaction, but I'd hardly call that a victory. I'd make a miserable *fille du joie,* or what-do-you-call-her, as Brita says, so I might as well get married." She tried to find a comfortable position. "Wrinkles and neuroses. Lebovitch told me, 'I wish sometimes you could be the man, at least for a fraction of a second!' 'Ah, it's lovely,' I told him. 'Aren't you overestimating being a male?' It's so sweet," Liza said sarcastically. "Almost every morning at breakfast, Munk claims that it isn't the only thing. I hope he's right."

It occurred to Dita that they were lying here like two naked souls.

"I've no regrets," Liza said. "My head is me; everything below the neck is only my body."

"Didn't it seem perverse to you?"

"Am I supposed to blame myself?"

"Then why do you do all those things for him?"

"It makes him happy, that's all."

"You told me once that boys don't want it that way."

"They do, but not all the way. You're still inexperienced in some ways. A person does lots of things without really knowing why. That's just one of them. All I'm afraid of personally is ugliness, that I'll stay poor like a churchmouse, or . . . I think that's all I'm afraid of."

Dita didn't answer. She wondered whether it wasn't a sacrifice women had to make. But she wasn't exactly sure what she had in mind.

"It's something else," Liza told her. "You've heard about how some opera singers drink raw eggs? Or about Japanese fishermen who eat raw fish when they're out to sea, and sometimes their wives and children back home do too, along with the roe?"

They could hear Brita breathing. The room was dark.

"There's a mystery about it even when you get used to it," Liza went on. "It's as if you can get used to something long before you really do it."

Again Dita avoided answering, but Liza hardly paused.

"I always wonder when I'm doing it whether I'd want it that way too if I were a man," Liza whispered.

Dita couldn't understand why she felt it would be better to keep her own experiences secret. She finally asked, "Don't you feel like an animal who's forced to submit to some other, stronger animal?" She felt sorry for Liza and didn't know why.

"People have always done it," Liza said, as if she were the judge and the accused at the same time. "Only nobody talks about it very often. And it's not the only thing kept hidden behind thoughts, even by those who are closest to you. Did you ever hear about the artist who painted one kind of picture for the popes and cardinals and another kind for himself? One of the paintings shows a man's head and what's in his mind, and that's it. Kings and priests or rabbis may forbid it, but people keep on doing it. It's like a taste. You've got to experience it for yourself. Taste can't be described. Nobody can do it for you."

"I don't know," Dita said, feeling accused. "I thought a lot of things were going to be different than they are. Isn't it as if somebody gave you a choice between food and poison?"

"It goes to a certain point. Then it seems like a lot. And then it doesn't even touch me anymore."

"Someone said that a woman is emptiness and that it's a man who fills it. But then it isn't man but woman who represents fullness. Woman as emptiness and fullness at the same time. That's not bad, is it? I wish I knew who said that first."

"It only goes deep, it never goes high. It's like dying. The most beautiful sleep is always the deepest kind. Sleep goes downward. It never takes you very high, like Tonitchka's screaming. What can you do about it?"

For a moment they were silent.

"You can always turn on the gas valve or grab a high-tension wire," Dita said. She had a lovely smile. And as carefree as she was, you could see and hear that despite her old irony, she believed this even more than she used to. Perhaps she believed it all the more as she grew increasingly remote from her own past.

"What about pills?" Liza asked.

"Who wants to ruin her stomach with pills?"

"As Brita says," Liza murmured into the darkness, "you've got to be perfect, but at the same time you mustn't look too experienced, so they don't get any ideas about you and lose respect for you. You've got to be a magician. But with our boys, if nothing else, you can at least be sure they're clean." Still, there was an undertone of doubt in Liza's voice. "A girl can never be sure."

Dita was thinking that not just Liza's children, but her children's children and their children and so on and on, years ahead, would feel the echo of what had happened to the great-grandmothers they'd never seen. And then she was thinking that maybe people first invented an omnipotent god to protect them, and then blamed him because he failed to do it, when in fact they had failed first. She was also thinking about dignity and how much of it had been killed. She thought about words like "courage" and "timidity," "confidence" and "suspicion," and those funny words "celebration of cowardice."

"You wanted to say something?" Liza asked.

Dita was listening for purity in her voice. "Why?" she asked. But her question was addressed to herself too. "I was just thinking," she went on, "about the darkness. At night controls are loose. You can lie better at night. Do you think Hitler is still alive?"

"You mean as if he didn't die at all?" Liza asked, really surprised.

"No. I'm thinking about what it means to be a woman." But what she was really thinking about was something inexplicable, something that had happened in the war, why it happened and why neither she nor anyone else could understand it. There was always that inexpressible mystery which seemed to her to grow deeper, higher, and wider the more time that passed.

"Everything's like the weather," Liza said. "In some, love brings out the best, in others, the worst, and in me, both. I didn't invent it."

"My aunt Mimi killed herself when the Germans came to Prague in 'thirty-nine," said Dita. "She jumped out of a window. She thought people were either greedy or else they just didn't care. Her grandmother committed suicide too. But I can't tell you why she did it. Nobody knew. Sometimes she'd sit for days on end looking out the window, and you couldn't get a word out of her. She could hear the soldiers marching over the cobblestones and she drew her own conclusions. Life had lost its dignity for her; there was no reason for her to live. Nothing mattered to her anymore. Not even herself."

"Maybe there's nothing wrong with that."

"My mother and father never talked about it. Not in front of me, anyway. But after a while I realized what had happened. I left as a child, but when I came back, I wasn't a child any longer. Then, from the few remarks I'd overheard, it suddenly emerged out of the darkness, like the iceberg that destroyed the *Titanic.*"

She remembered her Aunt Mimi, and how it had hurt her to see that people fought the Germans mainly with indifference. Mimi had been tall and thin, with blue eyes.

"The best thing I got out of the war was when I was in Theresienstadt taking care of the children," Dita said. "Who would have thought it?"

Both of them were almost invisible now in the darkness. The room was quiet. Dita thought of Aunt Mimi trying to catch chimeras. They always escaped her, just as her grandmother had, and then one day she jumped after one of them and the sidewalk was a long way down.

"You know," Liza said all of a sudden, as if she sensed what Dita was thinking about, "at first, I really thought it would be easy to forget. I'm not one of those people who remember only the bitter parts. Andy Lebovitch says that if we'd only wept in the camps, as a few people are doing now, and tried to figure it all out, it wouldn't have been just six million, but eight or nine million of us."

"Do you remember last spring when old Fatty told us about those ninety-three girls at the Jewish school in Warsaw who committed suicide rather than be selected as whores? It never was clear to me if it was for soldiers, imprisoned Germans, Poles, or prominent Jews. Do you know what I mean? I can see them in front of me the moment they were ordered to take a hot bath and then when they took off their clothing."

"Why?" Liza asked.

"You know what's really funny? The best people I ever met I met in camps. The longer I live, the more I see it that way. Right now, I feel that if I scratch all my memories of those times in Theresienstadt, Birkenau, or Bergen-Belsen fifty years from now, I'll find that they really were the best and the most important years of my life."

"My maxim is: No self-pity, no memories," Liza said. In the

shadows she looked like something between a nymph and a badger. "Self-pity is tedious and memories are boring."

Dita kept silent.

Then Liza said, "You know what I found out? That even memory is crippled if my present is invalid. That it's not true that we can take relief in our memories. If my present life is crippled, then my memories are crippled too. And even my hope is crippled."

"It's possible," Dita said.

"What are you thinking about?" Liza asked.

"About three women who by some gift of fate and their own will managed to change their destiny. One was beautiful, the second wise, and the third was strong."

"Sometimes I think about my father," Liza said. "Somebody told me that he worked in a Jewish *Sonderkommando* at Crematorium Number Four in Birkenau, where there was that mutiny in October of 'forty-four. But who knows whether it was true or not? Or if somebody was just trying to make me feel better? I asked everyone who was in charge of the morgue or the oil burners or the warehouse. Nobody knew for sure." She said it like a fly whose wings have been torn off.

"I can't agree when people who weren't there say it's impossible to put it into words, to give it meaning," Dita said. She could not give up the hope that everything people have done— even the most perverse things—could be described. "The sense of a word may shift, but I'm not afraid that reality will evaporate like mist. Every reality—fortunately and unfortunately, as Mr. Goldblat says—can be put into words. And one day not only will words get their meaning back, but things will too."

In the room the darkness had become transparent and comfortable. Through the open windows the sleeping city was crossed by stripes of shadow, like the touch of invisible fingers.

Liza kept silent. She had on an ivory nightgown with shirring and lace.

"It isn't true that after Auschwitz-Birkenau beauty can no longer be extracted from what's happened," Dita went on. "It would be a lie even if it were true. It would be too comfortable. Or something worse than that." But she wasn't so sure anymore. She didn't go on, and Liza didn't question her.

"I believe that maybe someday there will be a poem or a song, a statue or a book, for every one of those people who deserves it," Dita whispered later. She seemed to be part of another world, another girl.

"They're more likely to make a statue of Hitler first."

"I know it sounds stupid."

But still Dita thought that there should be the finest songs, poems, statues, or books that there could be. She could feel it in her bones that the only answer was for somebody to forge something out of the worst of it, something beautiful and solid as a song. But instead she said, "Do you believe in fate?"

"I don't waste time with such thoughts anymore," Liza said.

"I guess I believe in fate. I've been a fatalist for as long as I've lived. But actually, deep down inside, I don't think my fate will be so bad. Or am I just wishing it'll be that way?"

There was always something, whether they spoke of it or not, that Liza didn't tell, thought Dita.

Liza, reading her mind, laughed in the darkness. "Men, for God's sake! You sit around drinking lemonade with somebody for hours, having a lot of fun, and suddenly he starts looking at you very seriously, for no reason at all. As if something's snapped in his brain. Like an absolute idiot. He just goes on gaping at you. That's what's called 'desire' in better circles, or 'yearning.'"

Brita was snoring noisily.

"Do you ever think that someday you're going to have a baby?" whispered Dita, but she didn't expect an answer. "We're still young," she added. She touched Liza's hand. Liza's skin was rough and cold.

While Dita caressed her, Liza murmured, "My breasts don't amount to much, but I don't even mind anymore."

Dita felt a sudden clutch of pain in her abdomen, almost like cramps. It was coming late, as a punishment. Then, feeling a scummy heaviness under her belly and the sensation that her blood circulation was being reorganized, she began to describe in great detail the Hotel Astoria/Novak, formerly the Yellow Stone Inn, and the room.

She described the flowers in the window boxes, the double bed, the chaise longue, the curtains, and the kindling beside the stove.

But she didn't say a word about D. E. She gave a description of today's companion. Gold teeth, double chin, white cuffs, and gold cufflinks. She subtracted twenty or thirty years. She went into the most intimate detail. What happened next, what she thought, what was rough and what was gentle and how it changed from one second to the next, like when you snap your fingers and friendship turns into a love affair and you snap them again and there's just a bond of friendship and perhaps not even that. Things that perhaps do not exist. And finally the baby in the next room.

"It was laughing or crying," she whispered. "Later we saw its mother downstairs in the garden restaurant. A nineteen-year-old girl in a black sweater sitting with the waiter. The girl was very pretty and healthy and content. And so was the child. I can't describe it. I've never seen anybody who looked so blissful in all my life."

She'd mingled truth and lies. She didn't understand herself. But she felt better being where she was. Didn't the girl in the garden worry about what she was going to dream of? About what would happen to her child, her husband, her mother? About the future, present, and the past as well? Did she think about who needed her and whom she needed? And about how to manage her life? Did she feel from time to time like a dead tree, its roots cut, that depends on many circumstances in order to grow again? Don't people like that—compared to the other kind—resemble such choked-off crippled trees? Aren't they half dead too?

Brita was awake. "Who were you really with?" she asked. "It's O.K., if he loves you. But it's not often someone takes you to

131

a hotel room a second time for ten minutes of real business and two hours of crazy talk."

It was only then they noticed that Tonitchka was lying beside the Holy Virgin, curled like a deer beside an elephant. She hadn't closed her eyes the whole time.

"You know, when it happened to me for the last time in the war, it was with two soldiers who were in charge of the transport," Tonitchka said. "They took me into a compartment, chased the other women away, locked the door, and started to take off their uniforms. When they were in their winter underwear I didn't know what to do. I was scared. Then I started laughing. It was the first time I had laughed under such circumstances. And they got angry and left. Perhaps it is good to laugh at the worst."

"Let's make our gentlemen eat it themselves for a change, at least once!" grumbled Brita, but there was laughter in her voice. It was a sleepy, lazy voice like Alexander Lebovitch's. "Let them taste it as if they were giving you fine brandy, mouth to mouth, if you know what I mean. The first time I really liked it. He took a sip but didn't swallow it, and when he kissed me he gave it to me. So it's exactly like that."

In a little while they were all asleep. Sounds of the early summer night sifted through the open window, like a path "from somewhere to somewhere else," or else like the wind blowing across the green surface of a distant lake.

7

On Monday, June 30, the day of his marriage to Liza Vagnerova, Mr. Gotlob, wearing a blue marengo suit with a snow-white shirt and light gray tie, was the envy of all the boys from 24 Krakovska Street. He carried his Borsalino hat and calfskin gloves.

"He looks like a waiter on Sunday," Dita observed to Tonitchka. "But what can you expect? He thinks just because he's got money there's nobody in the world better than him. Imagine waking up in the morning with a bald head beside you."

At five minutes to eleven the car that belonged to the I.B.W. Student Union picked up Liza Vagnerova and drove her to the city hall.

Everybody from Liza's office had gathered around the boss, Mr. Zoltan Traubman, including the bookkeeper, his secretary, the law clerk, who was an Austrian citizen (and to whom certain laws and amendments did not apply), and the tax specialist whose services Mr. Zoltan Traubman would have been unable to afford anywhere else.

Mrs. Perla Traubmanova stood apart, like the wife of an Arab vizier. She came from Rumania, where Mr. Traubman had done business with dealers in cattle and horses.

"He's giving Liza a present. He's still got plenty of money," Tonitchka whispered.

"When a man's stingy, that's the first sign for me to call it quits," Brita said flatly. She was thinking about the fact that Liza was going to marry a man who was never in the camps as she had been. Was that good? Or just the opposite?

Dita was wearing the smile she reserved for gala occasions. She stared at Brita as if she couldn't believe her eyes. "How come you're wearing my scarf?"

"Why not?" retorted Brita. "Such things should be worn so they're worth twice what you paid for them, no?"

The adults stood in clusters, Munk in his winter coat, Fitz with a bowtie like a floppy propeller. Someone whispered that the hunched little man with thick glasses was actually Mr. Jacob Steinman, "former ambassador" and "friend of young people" and now general trustee for minors of the Council of the Jewish Religious Community. D. E. joined Dita in front of the stained-glass window.

"You'll be leaving for Switzerland next week. Did they tell you already? It's a summer study grant."

"Thanks, D. E. I know you had something to do with it."

"I'm not collecting any gambling debts."

The corner of her lips lifted. She was feeling fine, as she always did in a place full of people where you could laugh and gossip.

The boys who turned up were considered the elite of the Jewish students.

Liza was wearing a long taffeta gown with ruffles in front. Her hair had an auburn tint, thanks to a few drops of peroxide, and was combed in a smooth pageboy. A white lace veil fell from the pillbox hat and covered her forehead, her sharp nose, and her thick mouth.

"Everything that's beautiful is probably moral," Dita said.

"I'm taking the train for Paris on Thursday," D. E. told her.

I have one problem, Dita was thinking. It was that missing dimension that completes in a person the feeling that tells him he's living life to the full. Or like a four-motor plane flying on just one engine, which the black-haired boy from the kibbutz had talked about.

"In this world, whoever pretends to be objective is a crook, rather than objective," Brita said in her lazy voice.

The clerk led them into the hall, where they formed two loose triangles. The place was like a steam bath. Flies buzzed while two photographers clicked away. (Mr. Gotlob had ordered only one.) The flies beat their tiny wings and banged their blue-gray bodies against the windowpane, then staggered backward and buzzed around the room.

The bride and groom exchanged rings. Once, while still in Great Britain, Mr. Gotlob had commanded an honor guard during a visit from Lord Beaverbrook. When his lordship approached, he'd snapped to attention and bellowed orders like a lion. Now it looked as though the clerk had replaced his lordship and Liza Vagnerova was there in place of the honor guard. The wedding guests played the curious bystanders while Mr. Gotlob threw back his shoulders and poked out his chest, as if, standing at attention in front of a whole platoon, face to face with Lord Beaverbrook, he were taking a deep breath in order to issue his command: "Present arms!" or "Right face!"

"Being happy equals being sensible. Those qualities are indirectly proportional," Dita whispered.

She looked around at the windows of the wedding hall. She and D. E. made a handsome pair, both a head taller than the other wedding guests.

"After all, every army needs bookkeepers. Even the Germans," she murmured to D. E. "You can't win or lose a war without them."

Somebody said that an office for hunting down war criminals should be set up in some neutral country. Then maybe someone would find, in addition to the war criminals, all that Jewish–German–Swiss gold. Otherwise it will just revert to the bankers, who are rich enough already.

It was time to congratulate the bride and groom. Mr. Traubman leaned toward Liza. "Dear Mrs. Vagnerova-Gotlobova, just help yourself while it's there for the taking. The way things are now, the time is coming when the state is even going to take an interest in Rumanian cattle, import-export, respectability, and taxes."

He looked like Nostradamus four hundred years ago, predicting forty years of war and revolution, a world led by brainless idiots, and the destruction of everything.

"It's something different from scrubbing floors in some kibbutz," Brita observed.

Without even glancing at D. E. or Maximilian Gotlob, Dita added, "He always seems to feel yes-yes when the woman says no-no."

"Sour grapes," sighed Brita. "Are you supposed to be some sort of detective, keeping track of the difference between a mistake and love—as long as it isn't something else? It always goes from passion to stretching out and relaxing after a good meal."

"After all, we've got to know how to help ourselves in times of need," said Dita to the new bride. "I see happiness and love in your cards, Mrs. Gotlobova." They looked at each other.

"Everybody needs some kind of insurance," Liza replied.

"Tell us what it's like afterward." Holy Virgin grinned.

"I hope I won't need anything anymore," Liza whispered.

The wedding banquet was in the Hotel Sroubek in the middle of Wenceslaus Square. Mr. Gotlob had obviously spared no cost. It was noon; everybody was hungry.

"Ladies and gentlemen," he began, after he'd had a bit to drink. He lifted his plump white hand, like a policeman at the center of a crossroad. "When I lost my platoon in France that time, I never imagined that my lifeline would lead me into this port we call matrimony."

Waiters came in and took their places.

"Bravo." Mr. Zoltan Traubman applauded.

Mrs. Traubmanova was wearing black net gloves that reminded Dita of their late "delousing doctor" in Theresienstadt. The room was big and dazzling, filled with well-dressed people, waiters, and musicians. Five minutes later Mr. Traubman sang an old Hungarian love song for Mr. Maximilian Gotlob, "There's Only One Girl in the World for Me." Then, stimulated by applause, he sang a Transylvanian folk song and made a face like Dracula, with his great lovely genuine gold teeth. On someone's request, the musicians interrupted Mr. Traubman's Rumanian song with the antediluvian Russian "Dark Eyes." Afterward they played "There Are No Sunsets Above Granada" especially for the bride.

Andy Lebovitch had to promise Liza he wouldn't get into a fight with the waiters or musicians as he usually did everywhere lately, especially in the Rumania Bar. Maximilian Gotlob grinned as if the boy they had known in the winter had changed not at all during the spring—and now it was already the beginning of summer. He ate with pleasure.

Dita had been seated next to D. E. Mr. Traubman cast a few significant glances in her direction. She asked D. E., "Do you know the Japanese poem that goes like this: 'People say of us that we are secretly in love. I don't know how you feel about it, but my heart breaks that they are wrong'?"

D. E. smiled. "The verse, written on water?"

After the hors d'oeuvres and noodle soup, there were chicken drumsticks to nibble. Mr. Gotlob selected the nicest pieces of breast and leg for Liza. He drank a lot. He broke a cup and gave everybody a piece for luck.

"They gave the Congress scholarship for the Sorbonne to somebody else," D. E. said to Dita. "But I've got the trip all sewed up."

Dita didn't reply. She just tried to smile. The waiters started bringing in strawberries with whipped cream.

"Everything's starting all over again," said Brita. "It always does. Yesterday a boy told me that if I wasn't faithful to him he would have to burn the bed and buy a new one."

Dita asked Brita why she too liked strawberries so much, and loudly enough for Mr. Gotlob to hear.

"Look, this is how you eat a strawberry," responded Brita. "First you take the strawberry on a teaspoon and then you put some cream on it. Ah, the cream is so sweet. Then you put some more on it. You lick your lips because you like the taste. Then you open your mouth wide and put it in. O.K.? And that's the way you do it."

"Why does every wedding remind me of a funeral?" Andy wondered.

"A person's always his own executioner, more than anyone else." Brita looked at Mr. Gotlob.

"You have a beautiful gold ring," Tonitchka said to Liza.

"I am rich," Liza replied. Mr. Gotlob grimaced.

"Revenge is sweet," remarked Andy Lebovitch.

This makes no sense, Dita told herself finally. Everything in my life that has been true and good has always happened only once. Repetitions were never very successful. Was D. E. scared by what she had revealed to him in bed, that he had been the first man in her life, but that she would by no means be the last woman in his?

The musicians were playing tunes for almost everybody who requested one and for Dita they played "Ti-pi-tin" in an old-fashioned way, like the record with the Andrews Sisters. As a joke, Liza was telling Tonitchka what her nicest experience in 1944 at Birkenau had been. At first Liza had been with her older sister. Her sister had sliced their bread. One slice was thicker. She told Liza to take it because she was the weakest. Liza began to shout. What difference did it make, for God's sake, whether somebody was stronger or weaker in 1944, younger or older, taller or shorter, when everybody was hungry, everyone cold, everyone lost? The older sister lost her temper and slapped Liza's face. "And now you eat!" she screamed. "You've got to grow!" And Liza, tears streaming down her face, ate the thicker slice of bread so she'd grow.

For a few moments Tonitchka dreamed about getting slapped by her relatives. The musicians were playing for her; and since the wedding feast was well under way, she immediately began eating a golden piece of chicken. She had tiny thin white teeth.

Dr. Fitz was in an excellent mood. He drank a toast to each of them, like a statesman at a banquet. In his toast to Dita he said, "You could have been the Queen of England if you'd set your mind to it."

Then he added, as though the two of them were the only ones in the room, "You know who you really are?" And without answering his own question, he went on: "As I see, each one of you can wait around for your prince to come and in the meantime go on living inside your castles in the air. You know one of the disadvantages beautiful women have? Nobody believes them."

"Only the first hundred years after marriage are difficult," someone told Mr. Gotlob. "The second hundred are no problem."

"Who knows what happens after death?" asked Tonitchka all of a sudden.

"You don't have to worry about that," said Andy. "You'll certainly be dead longer than you'll be alive."

He had beautiful brown eyes, and once he'd told Neugeborn that Fitzi had survived not because he was smart or particularly strong, but because he'd been lucky and because he was blond and had blue eyes. That, maybe subconsciously, the Germans left him until the last minute and then they simply missed their chance.

It was as if he was reminding them that they hadn't spared him anything, that he was the only one of all of them who had not only seen a gas chamber from outside, but also from inside.

Brita argued over the table with Andy that, before they got married, Jewish boys tended to prefer girls who were closer to being "that" than anything else. Not because they did it for money exactly. But because of their behavior and accessibility. Although, where men were concerned, she thought prostitutes always had an advantage.

"Nonsense," Andy said flatly. "You can bet that if I'd been born a girl, I'd try being a whore at least twice a week. After all, who doesn't want to sell himself for as high a price as possible?" But the expression in his eyes was challenging and plainly said he was glad he'd been born a boy.

"We all know too well Balzac's advice to young men to treat a woman as a slave while persuading her that she is a queen," Brita said. Her voice was dry, as if she'd bitten off each word. "At the start you look for things you have in common with someone else, and when you find them you're overjoyed. At the end all you see is what separates you.

"People like you proposition me every other day," she went on. "*That* kind. They'll sleep with anybody who's willing to share their body with them—part of their body. Just a fraction of it. Not to mention a bed and a bit of floor space and a shelf in the pantry."

Mingling criticism and compliment, she concluded, "Andy doesn't care how many children he has, you know? He'll love them just as much as the kids will love him, no? Anyway, you're selfish. How many wives do you expect to have? You're all selfish. Or aren't you?"

Andy never indulged in self-flagellation. He got along using the principle of not overestimating anybody, or underestimating them either. But to his credit, it had to be admitted that he never spoiled anybody's fun either, unless he had to.

"Aren't you pregnant by me by some chance?" He grinned.

"Pregnant? By you? That's all I'd need!" Brita replied. "I don't just do it with everyone. I don't stop at every station. But I'm not an express train, either."

"There's an awful lot of cowardice in the whole thing," Dita interrupted.

"Is losing shame cowardice too?" Andy grinned again.

"Or the inability simply to say yes or no, without the whys and becauses behind it all," Brita insisted.

Dita leaned over confidentially toward Andy, "Prostitutes are good, aren't they? The same light that shines on the feet of the madonnas is on the feet of the whores. The two are alike. You are one hundred percent right."

"Nobody is perfect. Even Noah forgot to take fish on his boat." Andy smiled.

Mr. Gotlob particularly liked the golden chicken skin, grilled to a crisp. He praised the food, the appetites, and the manners of the "younger generation," and he beamed happily. Mr. Traubman, next to his swarthy wife, was also busily eating.

"Won't you have another tiny bit of cheese, darling?" she asked him for the tenth time.

Zoltan Traubman was insisting that "Bookkeepers were and always will be the backbone of every army and of the world. Trade is the salt of life, and whoever denies it is a barbarian."

He turned his gaunt head toward Mr. Maximilian Gotlob. "And your trade, Mr. Gotlob, is the noblest in the world."

"It's an appropriate time to thank the parents of my dear bride," began Mr. Gotlob and lifted his glass full of dark red wine.

"Everything is more simple than simplicity. People want to live better," Dita said.

She toyed with the bracelet. It was a kind of mute speech. She realized that sometimes when she looked at Tonitchka she saw her own self when she was little and her parents had taken her around by the hand.

Liza had tears in her small green eyes, and they had turned a torpid gray. Mr. Gotlob comforted her. "Come on, Liza. No, darling . . ."

8

Holy Virgin dragged her English steamer trunk up from the cellar. The room and the whole house smelled of whitewash, eau de cologne, and burned food. It echoed with "Meadow-lands," the "Red Army March," and "Ti-pi-tin." "One night when the moon was so yellow . . ."

Liza brought back Dita's wedding present, a record of "Jeri-cho," because Mr. Gotlob didn't have a phonograph. The room was a jumble of the things Brita was packing—books and sham-poo, pieces of fabric and tins of food.

"Butter . . . milk . . . certificate," Dita enumerated.

"How can you remember where you live when you're always moving?" Tonitchka queried.

"We all think we're something special," Dita said. "Are we? Who knows?"

Sometimes she had a feeling that she was looking at people and seeing what was sprouting in their future. As if she could see far ahead to what they were destined to do or be. As if she knew about the difficulties they would have in their future long before they did.

"Sometimes things are very well organized in this world," she said to Tonitchka.

"Try telling that to someone. Nobody'll believe you anyway."

"How will I ever move all this stuff?" Brita groaned.

Brita had been trying vainly to spend the last two days in bed. But she could see it wasn't working. While Dita and little Tonitchka were trying to cram her clothes into the trunk, Brita's eyes were half closed and her skin looked like cottage cheese. Dita was humming. "The flag of Ascalona will fly over my grave for ages . . ."

"I'm going to have to stay in bed for at least a day," Brita announced. She went over to the window and drew the curtains so no one could see in from across the street.

"Who are you leaving behind?" Dita asked.

"I went with quite a nice boy for a couple of weeks," Brita answered. "But he understood me too well. That's probably the first thing that cools me off; for me that's a sure sign that my romance is coming to an end."

" 'Loving too much'?" Dita quoted.

"Is that honestly your theory?" Tonitchka asked.

"Do you really want to know what my theory is? That we're not prepared for anything."

"What do you mean by that?"

"Just because our parents may have had things tough and more things disgusted them than not, and just because the war came along instead of some long-expected reward, is no excuse at all. They drilled all the rules into me: Be good and fair and honest and so on. But when I really tried to be that way, they nearly went crazy, yelling at me like I'd lost all my buttons!"

"Why are you always so quick to throw your boyfriends over?" Tonitchka wanted to know.

"Instinct," Brita responded briefly. "You can't keep them for long anyway."

It sounded like an echo of what Brita had said in the springtime. "For me, too good is too bad. Men abandon their principles much more easily than women. They sell themselves at a price no woman would ever consider, except maybe in an emergency." But she also had said that having affairs made her feel more alive. And in her eyes was always a mixture of memory and anticipation.

"Don't you do it just so they can't do it to you first?" Dita suggested.

"According to Rabbi Loew, a well-brought-up girl always says she doesn't know when she doesn't know," Holy Virgin said. "You don't need intelligence to have luck, but you need luck to have brains."

Tonitchka nodded. For the cats, the trunk was an opportunity to tear at anything they wanted. After everything was finally stuffed inside, Brita began to pull things out again—although ten minutes ago she'd tried to make sure not a single stocking was lost—and started to hand out her clothes to the two girls.

Besides not wanting to deprive Brita, they could see for themselves that, to put it mildly, most of her things weren't in the best shape.

"It's as warm and cozy here as in Siberia," Tonitchka said.

"Come on, now," Brita protested. "You're really going to hurt my feelings. After all, I'm going to England."

But except for the red hot-water bottle and some blue lace underwear, Brita watched helplessly as everything was tossed back into the trunk in the same arc she'd pitched it out. Finally she surrendered. She lay on her back like a bug, propping her head on her hands.

Dita picked up one of Munk's books. She put it on top of Brita's trunk. "To Brita Mannerheimova, respectfully, Max Peskov, Prague, July 1947," she wrote on the flyleaf.

"Sometimes all of us have to 'do it,' and it's probably better to do it now and then anyway than not do anything at all," Brita said suddenly. "But you girls know I never did it for money."

Dita yawned. "Balzac says that God punishes the man who wants to buy for money what can only be given away free," she said.

"Of all the things in the world, the most important is not money or love or the truth, but something else," Brita said.

Brita looked at Tonitchka's underwear. Maybe she was comparing those small, delicate, and carefully chosen bits of color and ribbon with her own underwear, which was bigger and, perhaps because of that, more graceless in shape and color, less attractive.

"Our little doll-baby," said Brita.

They all remembered how Brita, particularly in winter and far into the spring, looked as if she'd been dragged fully dressed out of an old wardrobe.

"You've got to take everything lightly, that's the whole secret of living when you're a woman," said Brita.

"Why?" Tonitchka wanted to know.

"Because you probably find more lies and deceit and cunning in relations between a man and a woman than anywhere else, even though each alone might be a perfect angel," Brita replied.

"Don't two and two angels make four angels?" That was more than just a question.

"If I knew that, I'd get the Nobel Prize for mathematics and I wouldn't be going to England," Brita said.

Dita looked a bit surprised. She was wearing her favorite outfit: a three-button jacket and a peach silk blouse with a blue scarf knotted at the throat.

"You'll need to take something with you, won't you?" Dita asked.

Holy Virgin sighed. "Justice, justice! Who knows where it lives? Before I leave, I want to tell you what bothers me more than anything else. In order to survive, a person's got to be a chameleon."

9

The procession to the railroad station set out at nine o'clock in the morning. They went from 53 Lublania Street through George Washington Street and the park. Mr. Goldblat walked in front. Doris Lewittova, with her baby and Neugeborn, stayed behind in the custodian's apartment to look after the house. Almost everybody else from Lublania and Krakovska streets was at the station. Mr. Traxler had organized an "integrated" orchestra, conducted by Andy Lebovitch.

"The musicians are thirsty," Andy shouted.

Everybody helped to elevate the mood. The station attendants must have thought it was a college outing. But there were only two pieces of luggage.

Mr. Gotlob patted Brita on the back. "You go right ahead, Brigita. They can't expect us to lick the lash they beat us with."

Liza Vagnerova-Gotlobova was wearing her yellow lace dress. Mr. Steinman stood hunched in a corner of the waiting room. He had only a single tooth left and he never spoke, because he didn't want to lisp. Then the people from the Palestine and Emigration offices arrived.

Lebovitch sang loudly while the band played "They used to be so proud of me, but now they claim I was a beast . . ."

Herbert Lagus's burning cheeks gleamed. He was struggling to push his way through to Brita in order to get closer to Dita.

"There's just one world." Munk couldn't resist.

Zoltan Traubman looked at him as if he were an oracle who'd just said something stupid.

At last the train arrived. All at once Brita didn't know what to do with her hands. And suddenly it didn't matter what anybody said. Shouts, whistles, smoke, and words—it was all like a pause or an inaudible voice that can't be silenced. The first person Brita threw her arms around was old Lev Goldblat, pressing her huge bosom, the envy of all the younger girls, into the hollow of his sunken chest. Finally she embraced and kissed Munk, whom she'd never managed to like.

"It's not very far," she told Tonitchka. "Actually, I've been preparing for this for five years."

A cloud of white sweetish smoke drifted over them while the coaches were noisily shifted back and forth. Dita studied the belly of the locomotive. Tonitchka coughed. The sign on the side of the coach said, *Prague–Nürnberg. Prague–Paris.* There was a diner and a sleeping car.

"We'll meet at Marble Arch," shouted Mr. Gotlob. "That was my station during the war. Or Finchley Road, where the underground comes up. Don't forget to say hello to my friend Winston!"

He was rewarded by a salvo of laughter. "It's easiest to go away when you're fed up with things," he remarked. He smiled like a full moon.

"We'll meet by St. Wenceslaus's tail," Brita promised. Her round pimpled face already looked out of her open compartment window. She had her breasts propped on the sill.

"Let's hope there's an international express train like this waiting for each one of us," Dita said.

Lebovitch chuckled. "Prague. Belsen. Change trains."

The men grimaced listening to Brigita Mannerheimova promise Tonitchka, "I'll send you a beautiful bra, honestly, blue or white."

Mr. Traxler winked a signal at Lebovitch. The two orchestras—one familiar from parties at 53 Lublania Street and the other from dances in the gym at 24 Krakovska—struck up the "Radetzky March," which would have been forgotten long ago if it hadn't been for Fitz, Munk, and Goldblat. Then came their favorite, "La Trieste." "Lieutenant, oh, Lieutenant, just put it there, your carnation so pink and fair . . ."

It had been sung in Italy during World War I "when the soldiers held out along the Piave, up to their knees in water or wading through the blood of their enemies and their own blood." They knew it in Czech and Italian. It rang through the station as though a bunch of old army veterans were departing.

They all look much more mature than they really are, the custodian thought to himself. We are going in the same direction, but on two different tracks, each for himself. He was afraid they were all a little crazy. It wasn't obvious, but it was a kind of madness.

Brita kept her arms folded across her breasts. A moment later the train began to move. Suitcases were firmly in place on the rack above her head, their tags bearing her address at 53 Lublania as well as her new address: Shropshire, Parkeville, Madeley, Lelford.

"So long, sweetie!" Lebovitch grinned. "Come on and stick them out for us!" He cupped his hands before his chest.

"But look out for the pillars!" Dita shouted beside him.

"Don't say it's impossible to make it without love!" Andy yelled.

The wheels were rolling. They could still see Brita's proud breasts, her soft pimply face, the velvet dress with the white collar. They heard the clank of steel against steel.

Dita ran alongside the train. "Just don't die from it!" she called, referring to the time Brita had complained about how difficult it was to be a woman, and Liza had replied that her man had trouble too because he had to shave twice a day. The whistle of the locomotive was shiny and could be heard all around the station. It was an old station. The name had been changed many times, from Kaiser Franz Josef to Woodrow Wilson to Adolf Hitler and to who knows what else, and finally to Prague, the Main Station.

Dita smiled. Her eyes were tired. The wind ruffled her hair. She was wearing her light spring coat, and the wind blew against her collar. Tonitchka was coughing loudly. The wheels began turning faster. The choir from Krakovska, joined by people from the Community and friends, began to chant, "Brita, Brita . . . !" Dita stopped and stuck her hands deep into her pockets.

The locomotive entered the tunnel first, and finally the whole train had disappeared. Within a minute Brigita Mannerheimova, better known as Brita or Holy Virgin, was gone and those who hadn't known she'd lived here since the end of the war would know no more of her now than if she had never lived here at all.

10

Not far from the newsstand, Herbert Lagus turned to Dita. Behind their backs Lebovitch was telling Mr. Steinman confidentially that Linda Huppertova was in some international Irgun Zwa Leumi camp near Kosice in Slovakia, where she was "learning to shoot to kill."

"To shoot and not to miss," he explained. "Who needs a trimotor plane that flies with only one propeller? Things are going to get hot for somebody down there among the orange groves."

He had his new accordion slung over his shoulder, and he talked to Mr. Steinman as if they were old acquaintances. "You can bet that any husband of hers will either run away or commit suicide within a year and a day!"

Linda Huppertova had moved out that morning and left a message in the china cupboard for the custodian. He didn't have to be a handwriting expert to see that the same hand had written the earlier informant's note. She'd written it on lined paper torn from a school notebook, saying she didn't intend to go on looking at "injustice and unfairness that shrieks to high heaven."

Mr. Steinman didn't seem to be listening. Some people were going to the station restaurant for beer.

"There's a difference between slapping somebody else's face and getting slapped yourself, isn't there?" Lebovitch said. That distinction expressed his complete idea of Zionism almost perfectly. The name of the place where Andy was going to meet Neugeborn was The World War I Beer Joint. They had switched from a place called By the Thirty-Six Just.

"This all reminds me of how Mr. Rosenblatt and Mr. Cohen were traveling by train," Dita said. "As they left the dining car, Mr. Rosenblatt complained, 'God should punish them for charging such high prices!' 'He already has!' answered Mr. Cohen, and pulled two silver spoons from his pocket."

"My family simply doesn't believe there's any future for us in Europe," Herbert said. "After all our experiences. Both world wars started here. If anything happens again, we think it'll start here first. It's worth it to us to bet on El Salvador."

He smoothed his hair, although it was already quite carefully combed. When he talked about things he could put into words, he expressed himself quite clearly.

"People who head for the Big City just because they know how to use a comb?" she asked.

She felt the excitement pulsing through the boy at her side. He walked close to her, a tall young fellow with a thick mop of wavy red hair. A girl certainly needn't be ashamed to be seen with him.

" 'I like you, Rat Catcher . . . you must have been loved by

148

many women!' And now you should reply, 'I don't know, I can't remember.' Or words to that effect, anyway."

"I suppose she'll be better off than she would be here," said Herbert Lagus, to make conversation. His nervousness made him awkward in her presence.

"You think so?" She walked on, close by his side. "Is that really what you think, or are you asking yourself too?" She could feel the quickening of his breath as he screwed up his courage to ask her the same question he had, in various roundabout ways, asked her many times before. "No, let's not talk about it. Why spoil a nice day?"

"What are you thinking about?" Herbert asked.

"They say rich girls are practical," she replied.

After a moment she went on. "I don't know whether you're right about how strong I am, Herbert. Not everybody moves around like Brita. How would I find my local train to bring me back?" She was trying to avoid a direct response.

"Maybe you don't care for me as much as you think you do," she went on. "I'm beginning to think that people imagine a lot of things about me. And then everything changes."

"I want to keep in touch," he said.

"When are you leaving?"

"Next Wednesday."

"You're not wasting any time."

"It wouldn't make sense to."

"You're sure to find some pleasant company."

"As soon as you let me know, I'll send you a boat or plane ticket."

"There are so many myths," she said. "Like myths about safe continents and dangerous continents. Myths about changing the worst into something better and the better into something best."

"But it's true that here in Europe there was the greatest racist slaughterhouse of all time," said Herbert.

"It's true, but didn't it happen just because of those myths? Or with a great deal of help from them?"

He was silent.

"The myth of Jewish power on the one hand, and on the other of Jewish helplessness," she said. "In one myth Jews are weaker than fleas and just about as clean. In another the same people seem to be cleverly conspiring to usurp the whole world. The same person is simultaneously the weakest of the weak and strong enough to survive the inconceivable. But of all myths, the one that disturbs me most is the one about our Jewish solidarity. One People, One Destiny. The urge to wander from place to place. As Mr. Steinman put it, we haven't nearly as much power as our friends would wish or our enemies think. It's like the myths about the Germans. They're either all omnipotent or else they're all superdevils."

But that was not the thing he wanted to talk about with her. Who were actually her friends, he asked himself, and what did she mean to them?

"Maybe the Jews and Germans share some common myths," she said. "Innate advantage on the one hand, and an innate sickness on the other."

"Why are you so much against leaving?"

"It would mean an end to idealism for me."

Herbert hesitated for a moment, and she could tell how her words were sinking in. Suddenly she knew that she was right on this point.

"We shall see," she said after a while.

"It's hard to leave you," he said suddenly. "I'd like to sit down somewhere with you and talk about how to make a good life together. I really don't know what to tell you."

"Half of the trip you'll cry, and the other half you'll be looking forward to new things."

Herbert Lagus listened to her, but it wasn't her words he heard. He wiped the beads of sweat from his forehead.

"What kind of suitcases do you have?"

"Like Brita's," he answered.

"Brita must be around Dvur Kralove by now. But maybe I'm wrong. Geography was never my strong point. I adore the grass, though. And when I try to decide what I like best, it's always cactus that loses."

"It's a lovely day," said Herbert.

"We haven't had such a beautiful summer in years," she said. Everybody tried to look beyond tomorrow. That wasn't entirely wrong, of course. Except that something got lost that might have given a great deal of happiness right here and now. There was no question in her mind that there was nothing she could give to him, except one thing. There would always be some things she didn't want under any circumstances. But she couldn't tell him that she considered him sexless, as if he were a neuter or—to be kinder—like a younger brother. She would never be able to picture herself in bed with her younger brother. "Isn't it funny," she said, "how people like us always find some use for suitcases, no matter how long they are stored in the cellar or attic?" She could easily imagine the letters they would exchange before the summer ended. She decided to join Andy Lebovitch for a beer.

Lifting the corners of her mouth and tossing back her hair, she shook hands with Herbert. Just to make sure, she didn't even let him kiss her cheek.

11

On her way home to 53 Lublania, she stopped off at Josefovska Street. She could still hear what the landlady had told her right after the war: "So you've come back, Dita. Well, it doesn't matter." Mother had hidden away a few bath and dish towels with the woman. That was the day Dita had taken a streetcar to Lublania and three boys from the English Brigade had gotten on. One man had looked at her and said, "I bet you couldn't wait for these black-haired bastards to come back, could you?" And as she had walked down Lublania Street, some people were coming out of the tavern at number 51 and one of them had spat right in front of her. As though she'd turned his stomach. Who knows what she might have heard if she hadn't looked like a Scandinavian?

Sometimes it seemed strange to the people that all of them had not been burned in the ovens, that not all of them were turned into a piece of soap, as the newspapers had reported. In some synagogues the Germans kept horses during the war. This was the main reason why at least some buildings had survived. Andy didn't like people asking him, "You are still alive?"

The enterprising landlady had made an apartment out of the former laundry. And it never even occurred to her that they should move out because Dita had come back.

The door to the laundry that used to belong to Josef Sax and Vera Saxova had been bricked up. In a sense the same thing had been done to the year their daughter had spent in the School of Applied Arts, and to their own dreams of a white house and of a life that would have made it possible. It was the price they'd paid for their daughter to swim safely in deep water. I won't go. Why should I? What would I find there, after all?

The Vltava smelled of summer. It had been the loveliest spring she could remember. Summer seemed promising too. She was so superstitious that as soon as she had said it she told herself it probably wouldn't last. She recalled her favorite songs from Lublania Street and "One night when the moon was so mellow . . ."

It really had been a lovely spring. She knew why. The trees were not yet tired, the leaves were fresh and young and strong. She looked at the river. Wild ducks were swimming against the current, heading upstream from the weir where the water was clear green with white foam that floated off down the river. There is no sense in going, she thought. Why should she?

Then, standing and leaning against the street lamp, she wrote D. E. a letter:

D. E., I think I still love you. It took a long time for me to understand that if a man wants to go to bed with me, it doesn't mean he wants to marry me and that I don't necessarily need to hold that against him. And only recently have I been enjoying the discovery of another mystery—that not everybody who enjoys my company wants to sleep with me—which isn't so much their loss as mine.

It appears that my stars are still generous to me, and after the fat nights come the lean nights.

I don't know why I still feel so uncomfortable writing love letters. I probably should take Stendhal or Balzac as a model. But I know, as Andy does (even if he isn't your idea of the model of a man), that love, or whatever you call it, the kind of love I'm capable of and the kind I need—that kind of love you can only pay for with love. You only like strong people. Without self-pity. I hope to be strong enough someday.

You probably have your bags packed already. I hope you have a good trip. I've got a good imagination; I think up scenes where everybody plays a leading role and it goes on and on forever. But every "forever," every "eternity" scares me. Too bad I don't know how to cook. Next time we meet, I'll invite you up to my place and fix you something nice. Maybe by that time I'll learn to cook.

I also know by now that the less I say to you, the more willingly you listen. And that the closer I want to hold you, the farther you move away from me. Would I be the same way if I were a man? Would you try to cheer me up if I began to cry in front of you?

You really are like an iceberg sometimes. With other people, by knowing only a little about them, I know almost everything. With you it is different. Even though I know almost everything, I know only a little.

Every day brings with it what it must. I force myself to accept it, without thinking about it too much. As the dead rabbi from the Twelfth District once said, life is mystery and poetry, and what you need for an old melody is a new audience. Feeling has to be the most important thing in the world, at least for a while. Sensitivity and the ability to listen to what somebody else has to say. So talk to me!

Yours, Dita

She looked charming in the early summer sunlight, young and fresh, spoiled and yet unspoiled. Nobody should walk over a corpse, went the old saying, not even over his or her own dead body, she thought, and smiled.

The gulls, she thought, are like life itself. They hovered on the air, circled higher and higher, plunged suddenly to soar again. But the one thought that had taken firmest root in her mind, and against which she could find hardly any argument, settled and gnawed within her.

She stood there for a long time watching the river.

four

1

Nine months later Dita Saxova wrote her first letter from Switzerland. She enclosed a postcard showing the three-pronged peak
of the Wetterhorn, the sloping glacier with the bare stone spurs
along the top. She could imagine how Lev Goldblat would display it on the china cupboard.

I can just hear you say "the most ungrateful girl even to herself."
You must be asking why I went away.

The longer I'm here, the more good things I can see at home. There
are lots of people here with whom I have nothing in common and
even more I don't want to have anything to do with. The important
thing here is to have money, and people have to know what kind of
family you come from.

The house here has a 100-year mortgage. My God, that's ten times
ten years—a hundred years. Some people can actually still look ahead
a hundred years. Not only can they figure where the children of their
children are going to live, who haven't even been born yet, but how
and when they're going to pay the mortgage off and in what payments.

It occurs to me that nobody cares as much as I do about what will be now—right now. My *now* must seem ridiculous to people who've got the nerve to take out a bank loan for a hundred years. But if anybody asked me whether I envy them and whether I'd trade for their loans and property, I wouldn't hesitate a minute. I still want to get everything I can out of life now, right now, this very minute. It's probably true what the Italians say, that a person who moves from one place to another changes only the stars over his head but not his nature. They also say it's better to fall out of a window than off a roof. And that only what's new is lovely. And every affair has to come to an end. Brita can testify to that. I still have a few trumps in my hand. Some of them are up my sleeve. But the cards are always being dealt out, and what doesn't come today can always come tomorrow. So don't worry. Everything's all right. Just take it easy.

Last Monday I met a man from Poland here who has some American-Swiss business connections. It seems that he managed to escape from Germany to Switzerland during the war, only to have the Swiss turn him over to the Germans even making him pay for his own transportation to the border. He didn't know that the border was his destination, but rather thought that he was going to obtain work. That sounds somewhat familiar, like the situation of some of our people, doesn't it?

This is the end of the fasting. I've gained four and a half kilos, unfortunately not in my face, but at the other end. I take long walks, go to the theater, and eat food from the finest menus. I sit at the table according to protocol and dress according to the lastest fashion.

I think it is also the end of an idealism. Emigrants are like virgins in a dancing class. Very sensitive. Oversensitive. You must handle them with kid gloves. In that, they remind me of the sensitivity of old spinsters. Emigrants have a hard time of it here. It's harder to be a foreigner here than to be a Jew anywhere else. There's nowhere you can appeal, and you get no moral support. When a Swiss moves to another canton, he is just as much a foreigner as anybody else.

She had no idea that at the very moment she was writing the letter, old Munk was mailing her one from Prague, from the other end of the world. As usual, he wrote that he missed her and that he wished her all the best for her nineteenth birthday. And that even though he worried about her sometimes without knowing quite why, he had the same kind of faith in her that an older person has in someone who's already grown up. He went on to write that her life reminded him of someone who has built a fire from just a little pile of kindling, but is soon rewarded with brightly burning flames. He wrote about the dignity of life and how he couldn't believe that man's dignity had been destroyed forever because of what had happened during the last war. And he said that it is concern for the fate of our children that lies closest to our hearts. And, of course, that the world couldn't be so big that one person could lose another for very long.

In her letter Dita didn't mention the other side of the coin, nothing about how Mr. Zoltan Traubman had behaved at Ceske Velenice, the Austrian-Czech border checkpoint. He and his wife were escorting a group of undernourished Jewish children. When he found out that his luggage had not arrived, he lost his nerve. "I knew it all along!" he whispered. And off he went to hang himself in the lavatory. He was found in time and cut down, and he continued on his way in the best of spirits.

On the other side of the border a Swiss doctor complained about how badly behaved the Jewish children were. They refused to be vaccinated or to take the showers they were supposed to have before they got to Basel. The doctor complained to Mr. Traubman. "If they don't stop carrying on this way, you might as well go back to Prague. We'll be glad to take some German children instead."

In the meantime, while the children were in quarantine, one of them had asked a German boy, *"War dein Vater bei der Gestapo?"* and upon getting the answer *"Jawohl,"* had smacked him in the face. The Swiss had been quite unable to comprehend this. Many of them were deeply sorry for poor defeated Germany.

In Basel the group had been welcomed like long lost relatives. A reporter from the local Jewish paper had taken charge of her. She wore a tailored travel suit of soft English flannel. The reporter had asked her whether there were still Russian troops quartered at the Prague castle. An article came out about her.

Almost three thousand words, the reporter said.

"You're very pretty," he told her. "Blue eyes, golden hair. The Slavic type. Like a Swede." She didn't contradict him by explaining that the "Slavic type" is more likely to be brunette. He spoke of a modern Exodus. In her answers she accentuated the future. She thought about her mother's saying that only a fool tells everything. A normal person says only what's necessary. But her mother also used to say that a man is like a tree; he has a visible strength and beauty, like a trunk, branches, and leaves, and an invisible power, like the roots.

She told the reporter how strange it was in Prague after 1945 to pass a synagogue that hadn't been destroyed in the war, but which stood empty, without people, like an extinguished lamp or as if it had been gutted by invisible fires.

With a smile, she told him that only cats have nine lives, humans can expect only one. He liked that. She had even confessed to him her vision of "calm green lakes" and of the "path from somewhere to somewhere else," in an attempt to balance the light and dark sides of her words, as if here at last there might be some fulfillment.

He had laughed. He had had another kind of experience. He asked her what was most important to her. "To make a decision," she replied.

The meadows were fresh, and the soft colors of grass and flowers made everything look tender and fragile and firm beyond compare. Golden bees, black flies and shiny beetles, blue dragonflies. And mountains, very high and very strange, above all.

Her photograph with the smile that she had borrowed from the girl at the Hotel Astoria/Novak, formerly Yellow Stone Inn, appeared along with the article. She was wearing a new ruffled cotton blouse with embroidered flowers and leaves, white on white, which gave it a lacy effect. She received two copies in Grindelwald with a note asking her to acknowledge whether or not she had received them. Not a word about an honorarium. She smiled. I'm still learning, she said to herself. But in an hour or so I'll probably feel that even a smile is too much weight to bear.

It was snowing outside. She looked out the window at the three-pronged mountain and at the fourth peak, which was even higher. Something cracked inside the glacier. Sometimes she wanted to crawl up there in her shoes with the cardboard soles. She was sorry she hadn't brought along her portable phonograph and her old records and books; 53 Lublania Street was very much in her thoughts. Was Munk still distributing his books at Lublania like a salesman of lukewarm water? "I know, Dita, I know. The sickness of mistrust and loneliness is strongest in the handful of you who came back from the war and the camps too young to be left to your own devices and yet too old to suffer anyone to look after you."

She was playing with her bracelet. For Herbert, civilization and the consciousness of man were constantly improving. Words expressed all meanings clearly. And freedom was the easiest existence. Like the idea that thinking things through is safer than trusting instinct. Or that there is a beginning and end to all events. Or that man is the best of all creatures.

Why does everybody want to purchase his own security with the insecurity of someone else?

Last time, when they were dancing at the Cafe Phoenix, he'd told her about an earthquake that had shaken the bottom of the Pacific Ocean, far from shore, endangering buildings on the mainland as well as ships at sea. He took great pains to point out that his was another kind of danger, that it didn't have the advantage of endangering everybody equally. He spoke of an immense tidal wave, as high as the *Titanic.*

Sometimes when she woke up in the morning, she'd rub her eyes, get up, and look into the mirror, feeling as if her soul was in a thousand pieces, even though nothing was happening to her or around her. Then she could hardly understand how it was possible that her large oval face looked so clear and fresh. There were no circles under her eyes. She looked rested.

The room was empty now. The other girls had gone and the silence there seemed almost unfair. As if she were expecting the world to cluster around and begin to turn the way she wanted it to—at least partially. Sometimes she thought backward to when she'd been a little girl and everyone around her was talking about a pretty white house, a lake, surface of water leading off into the distance, a shore somewhere on the horizon, and a road that led "from somewhere to somewhere else." Her mornings were melancholy.

She remembered the time when she'd come back from her excursion with David Egon Huppert and Neugeborn had been waiting in the hall, as if by coincidence. He was smoking and he told her offhandedly that he'd been there to fix the water pipe so she'd be able to take a bath now if she wanted to. She remembered how she'd wondered what to say to him. Finally she told him she didn't owe him anything and there was nothing she hated more than when people gave themselves false hopes. He was whistling the song about the virgin and the whore.

The door of the ski room squeaked intermittently. The language course she'd just finished had also been attended by emigrant girls from Poland, Hungary, and Rumania. It was just like Theresienstadt between 1942 and 1945, when former cabinet ministers and secret counselors had boasted about how distinguished they'd been in the past, the more so as their old glory faded. The more insistently one of them tried to demonstrate the importance of his position in the past, the more fervently did he come to believe in it himself. Many were homesick, miserable, and two days out of three, mentally and physically ill.

She could almost hear the voice of old Munk. He assured her that she had nothing to lose, and that, after all, life gives everybody a chance, even if the chances aren't equal. It's too bad we can't quickly glue together what doesn't stick as well as we think it ought to, because time passes so fast. Too bad you can't run on ahead of yourself by at least a year. We just keep looking back at some things, while others we only allow ourselves to imagine. You've got to be strong. Suddenly she had a vivid vision of Prague, of a particular place down by the riverside on Kampa Island. She saw it not quite as a mother sees her child, or a child its mother; for she had not yet had a child, and she no longer had a mother. But it was there that she'd learned whatever those mysteries are that turn a small animal into a human being.

Her vision was compounded of her childhood, of the war, of the liberation and all the armies involved, of her life at 53 Lublania Street and the archives where she had worked, the school she had attended, all the people she had known before and after, what had happened and what hadn't. The songs were there too—a jumble all mingled together, yet she could easily single one out and play it over in her mind. The boys. All the young men she'd ever been interested in, and everyone who'd ever tried to win her favor. Andy, who had tried to seduce her once by telling her that he felt like a lonely animal in the jungle. And why that was not enough for her. And how often in only ten minutes they'd managed to arrange room 16 to look like a makeshift cafe, catering to the boys who formed a kind of elite among the Jewish students. She was thinking about the remarks of that young man who came to recruit people for the Promised Land (capital P, capital L), and how he had begun by telling them about the transit camps in West Germany, then spoke about his trips through Austria and Italy, and concluded with the fact that every emigrant would receive from the future Jewish government a bed, his first wages, and an unlimited stay in one of the ten camps in Palestine until he could "stand on his own two feet."

She might have added in her letter that she liked to walk up to Bachalpsee below the Faulhorn, where the water was as cold as ice, even in the summertime. She wrote, "It's been snowing all week and all morning, but I think it's about the last snow of the season. I must stop, or you will pay extra postage. Yours, Dita. Grindelwald, Morning, March 22, 1948."

2

An hour later it had stopped snowing. The radio from the Bort Chalet was blaring. She shrugged her shoulders defiantly, as though conducting an argument with someone. She took her envelope to the post office. The angular German letters reminded her that Berner Oberland would still welcome her.

The air smelled of snow and of the coming spring. More than ever the mountain looked to her like a woman. She thought about the quantity of rocks up there that had never been measured or weighed. She thought about the evening ahead. Mr. Jacob Alfred Wehrli, the man who had financed her language course, was giving a farewell party in his home.

As she gracefully dropped the letter into the mailbox, a blond crew-cut American tourist stepped up to her. "All alone, baby?"

"I think you've made some mistake," she said. And in Czech she added, "I don't think I'm what you're looking for, sonny." Her lips pouted a little, and her eyes were fixed on the rocks and forests high above.

From out of nowhere the American said, "Good luck to you," and disappeared.

There were two letters waiting for her in the hostel. The first had a huge red El Salvador stamp on it, and inside there were snapshots of a new house with a flat white roof and a renewed invitation. The second letter was from D. E. Inside was a fifty-franc bank note, folded twice, and a few lines describing his new goals in life and his farewell to the old. "Why should I exchange one ghetto for another?" Dita felt herself blushing. Her fingers trembled, and she'd torn open the envelope so fast she'd ripped off a part of his return address. My God, she thought to herself, I'm not. I know very well I'm not. It is the "in between the lines" that gets you.

Only ten days before that she'd written a long letter to D. E., but the letter was never sent, only the postscript.

She wrote him that to this very day she still didn't know what kind of an answer he wanted to hear (if he wanted an answer at all) that time when they came back from the hotel in the country, when she got out of his amphibious car on Lublania Street. She told him how long his parting words had rung in her brain. How finally she accepted them as a gallant gesture in a game that's been interrupted and which wasn't to have been continued anyway. How he'd acted the next time—as if they'd seen each other last just yesterday and had oceans of time ahead of them. It was as if this awakened something inside of her that had been asleep for a long time and of which she did not want to be reminded.

Of course she was hurt, like every woman who gets the brush-off—especially since she had the feeling that she hadn't been asking for all that much. She told him that it had gone so far that she almost began to go out of her way to insult him. And how something happened that she hadn't counted on, almost against her will. How after he left, her own departure was something between a defeat, an escape, and an act of defiance. Or was it the other way around? But I still keep wanting to believe, she wrote, that the world is well planned and organized. Those who stay alive always have the last word.

I am not, she kept repeating to herself. Maybe I look that way, but I am not.

3

That evening at the party that had been talked about for so long in advance Dita Saxova appeared in a new dress of pale blue taffeta, white gloves, and white shoes. Lately she liked to appear dressed all in Zionist blue and white, except for the black alligator bag she'd bought with her last bit of pocket money. It was a pretty dress. An Italian cleaning girl had helped her make it. In broken Italian, Dita had told her about how during the war she'd gotten a handmade bra, which at that time represented much more than just another piece of underwear. *Figlie a vetri sono sempre pericolo!*

She smiled and said hello to people she didn't know, and strangers smiled back at her. The ballroom was elegant and almost full. She overheard scraps of conversation: "Never? Never is a big word. It pretends to be, anyhow."

A young man in a blue blazer with gold buttons and gray English flannel pants reminded her of Neugeborn. "Somewhere they unearthed a prehistoric flea that had been petrified for millions of years," he was saying. "In New Zealand they found some dead whales that had swum into shallow waters, even though they must have known they'd perish. Whales do that now and then."

She looked at herself in the mirror.

"Nobody knows why," explained the young man. "They found a parasite in the ear of the leader of that troop of whales, a three-centimeter worm that might have disrupted his navigational ability. And sometimes a nursing baby will imbibe a fatal disease along with his mother's milk. There's no way of knowing beforehand." Then he looked around and said, "Why is it that some people always look as if they've been dead since last Tuesday?"

There was a young couple standing in the corner of the larger room. Dita heard the name and it caught her attention.

"Andy," the girl said. "I thought you went back to Austria."

"No, I stayed. Things became better after the races," the boy said. He had a thick chestnut-colored mustache.

"You met a woman?"

"Yeah."

"Oh, no. How old is she?"

"Forty."

"Rich? Married?"

"Yeah."

"How many kids?"

"Four."

"Oh, Andreas, why are you doing this again?"

Dita recalled that once Linda Huppertova told similar stories about her at 53 Lublania Street.

"Now I can understand why people are so frightened of going crazy." Dita smiled to her companion.

She was trying to find something, or to prove something to herself, but she didn't know exactly what it was. It made her a little bit nervous. Something was in the air. Tomorrow real life begins. On my own two feet, she said to herself. She felt refused—not only by D. E. but by the world, which she herself was refusing. It went deep and aroused only repugnance. It was not necessary to ask herself why.

She moved away from the mirror in order not to feel embarrassed if anyone were looking at her.

"Somebody said that what's true doesn't always have to be probable," the young man said. *"Le vrai peut quelque fois n'être pas vraisemblable."*

"Really?" She stood next to him. "Do you think there are at least ninety-three girls in this room?" she asked, looking around the big ballroom and the adjoining rooms.

"Do you like clean things?" he answered.

"Do you like whales?" she replied with an innocent smile.

He turned to her and with the same kind of smile replied, "I'm crazy about them."

Her look was half smile and half silent reproach. "Isn't it funny that in every language a person is someone different," she said in French.

He was looking around. "Fortunately nothing human is doomed from beginning to end to destruction, and only animals feel how alone they are," he said and smiled. "Have you ever awakened in the middle of the night and out of nowhere felt sweat all over your body and found yourself trembling in fear?"

"You must be out of your mind." She smiled.

Near them danced a couple in perfect formal evening clothes. Looking around her and trying to get into the mood, she found herself thinking about the letters in her handbag, about shame and courage. About the vain try to be happy in some lasting way and why it makes one appear to be a lost soul and not know why. Nor does anyone else know why, she said to herself.

The chandeliers glittered. The rooms were full of flowers. Outside the moon was shining, and the tops of the hills were full of chalky white snow that lasted through all four seasons. Close to the house there were tall and slender pine and fir trees swaying slowly in the wind.

Someone was making a speech in front of the reception room. In her mind she was closing the gap between the echoes of 53 Lublania Street and what was being said by the short fat man in a plaid waistcoat, a Sudeten German. "We will return to our places at home, ladies and gentlemen."

Someone was saying to a very nicely dressed girl, "You are so pretty."

"What good does that do?" the girl replied. "It won't feed me or pay the rent." She smiled briefly. "I want to be happy. It must be possible to be happy." And then, "Do you know what it means to be wealthy? Freedom of choice."

The man said, "Money makes it easier." They danced away.

Two men in salt and pepper tweed suits were sipping whiskey at a table with an Aladdin's lamp and roses in a Chinese vase. One of them was saying, "Her husband screamed one night, 'Damn, you won't shake that mother's ghost of yours!' It had taken her twelve years to get her mother's ghost out of the bedroom, all those nights when her mother's shadow fluttered at the foot of the bed. 'How can anyone concentrate on making love to you,' her husband said, 'when you take everyone into the bedroom with you?' She stared back at him and asked, 'Doesn't everyone?'"

The young men looked at her, judged her, smiled at her, and one said, "Some people seem to have the instinct of migratory birds. They hardly touch the ground. Most of the time they are in the air."

Suddenly she remembered, without knowing why, how it was when she finished kindergarten and was supposed to start first grade next year. Wasn't it like wanting to cross a river and not seeing any bridge because there was no bridge there? Today she was finishing something that meant childhood and set off echoes of it, no matter whether she'd get what she wanted or not. Tomorrow she'd draw another invisible line through what she'd never get. Maybe her children would, providing she'd ever have any. And I might, she realized.

She thought of all the things that might have spoiled her but hadn't. On the contrary. And so things changed, but something fundamental remained. Like an anchor that floats along with the ship, on the same chain. What value has the life of one single person? Practically speaking? For many people someone else's life means almost nothing. Sometimes it doesn't even mean much to the person himself. But he's got to be alone for a long time before he finds that out. Or else he's got to have been unlucky for a long time and not have succeeded in anything he's aimed at.

"Life is short," she said to the young man in the blue blazer.

"Fortunately," he added with a smile.

"You like fairy tales, don't you?"

"Yes, but not the German ones with cruel endings." Dita laughed. "It's a pity that most German fairy tales end badly."

The young man really reminded her of Neugeborn. All the rooms were full now. The musicians started to play again. The fat man talked about the cleanliness of Western civilization, about the need to protect its purity just as devotedly as in the house of Torquemada. He spoke in French.

"You have a nice bracelet," the young man said.

"Thanks."

She really had two souls. She had listened to the old fat Munk. She heard him tell her that he was preparing himself for spring. The snow, he told her, will melt soon. She smiled. The young man didn't understand it.

She looked over at the sons of their host. They were identical twins. Their mother was a platinum blond. "Your boys look wonderful this evening, Mrs. Wehrli," someone told her. "This is a most admirable thing you're doing."

Dita waited for the introductions to end. It was different from night clubs and theaters and parties in Prague; but, as a matter of fact, everything was different—and not only in size. The two letters she had gotten that afternoon had a bearing on each other. D. E. had already worked himself into a job at the headquarters of the International Blue and White Student Union. The bank note he'd enclosed was like an inadequate bandage laid on the laceration of his announcement that by the time he'd gotten her last letter, he had been "happily married for all of two hours."

"Would you like some wine?" the waiter asked her.

She helped herself and strolled through the drawing room with her crystal goblet. Another waiter approached her. "Some dessert?"

"No, thank you," she replied and ran her hand down over her hip. The tall young man who resembled Neugeborn winked at her from across the room. She walked toward him with a swaying motion. Dancing had started in the middle room. She put her handbag on a little table near the window where brocade drapes were held back by a fringed gold cord.

The young man twirled her into a waltz. "You dance very well," he said. She only smiled.

"Is everything spinning as fast for you?" he asked.

"It makes me dizzy," responded Dita. She closed and opened her eyes. The effect was somehow very appealing. "And it's not a wheel, it's a river, flowing fast, and I don't know where it's going."

When the dance ended, the young man escorted her to the table where she had left her purse. She picked it up. The purse had a pleasant shape, like a horseshoe.

Between the dances waiters brought around crystal cups of almonds, raisins, oranges, and bananas mixed with a sauce made of egg yolks, cottage cheese, and sugar.

After reading what D. E. had written, Dita had mentally composed and sent a "message full of love and humility" to Herbert Lagus. At the same time she realized that from the start there had been two D. E.'s in her life. It was as if she had two lives too.

A soprano from the Bern Opera was singing a Swiss folk song about a path in summer. The singer stood in front of the microphone in a close-fitting green silk dress.

One of the paintings on the wall reminded Dita of the reproduction Munk had given the girls in room 16. Brita had dropped it in the oven last winter. Its title coincided with the song—"A Summer Morning."

She didn't know which vision, each drawn from reality, to reject first. Her cheeks were flushed from the wine, the closed rooms, and the presence of so many people. Her eyes shone and her body swayed as she moved across the thick Persian rug with its intricate pattern of serpents, birds, and trees.

She listened to the singer. Every time she thought of herself and D. E., she couldn't help feeling that experience lying somewhere at the bottom of her mind. Or as if she were listening to some familiar song in which her voice played an inconsistent and disappearing part. There was fear in the song for something she thought would have no place in her future. D. E. seemed just as guilty as he was innocent, and she too seemed simultaneously guilty and guiltless. Of course there were also two Dita Saxovas. She tried to smile and found that it wasn't so difficult after all.

D. E. had bought a Renault sports car, but, he wrote, it couldn't be compared to his old KDF amphibian. He had said "goodbye to sentimental memories, which could only interfere with the concentration that is essential to the tasks confronting the new generation today."

It was sincere and pompous at the same time, like everything about D. E. He didn't need to mention that "he had resolutely turned his back on the past and broken off an already infrequent correspondence with his stepsister" or how much "more mature" he felt than French people of his "generation."

Finally, he wrote, everybody, regardless of what he says or how he behaves, is prejudiced—by himself to start with, and then by property, career, status. Because that's man's nature and it'd be a lie to deny it or to feel guilty about it. He assured her that no matter what happened, they'd remain friends, no matter where they were.

She could just imagine how he would behave if they ever met here. Would she act flighty and a little crazy, laughing loudly, feigning both forgiveness and bitterness to conceal her memories, her feelings, and her thoughts—and would she press his hand?

The letter she had written ten days ago expressed things he would never know, because she still had the letter with her. Now she went over the same thoughts, even as she listened to the music or danced.

She felt as if she were floating down a stream and getting farther and farther away from people she didn't want to lose. But she kept smiling and looking elegant and content, exactly as she had to.

So D. E. had eliminated her for good from all his plans for the future. One thousand percent. But she still thought about what it would be like if he were here, now that it would also mean the presence of his new wife and perhaps his father-in-law. D. E. would be jealously protective of her, even if the poor thing couldn't take a step without her cane. And he would forgive her father anything, even being a munitions maker.

Dr. Fitz had once told Brita about the farmer who was plowing a field when a thunderstorm came along. The lightning struck the plow, and within a second the farmer experienced all the horrors an unprepared person feels when the end of the world seems to be upon him. But he lived through it, and the next time he was prepared. The next time there was a thunderstorm, the same thing happened, but it didn't upset him. Anyway, the same thing doesn't always have the same result. What had Dr. Fitz been trying to tell her with this story? Did she wonder with whom he'd been talking about her? Yes? Or no?

It was all so different from the green-clad soprano from Bern. Strength flowed into her from David Egon Huppert—and perhaps it had little or nothing to do with his character. Nor was it simply a result of some mutual presence or physical contact.

Maybe the same kind of strength even flowed from her into Herbert Lagus. Who knew?

She looked around her and felt coils of heat encompassing her. She knew that when a person feels poor, everyone else seems rich. The mirrors everywhere were returning her smile back to her. She felt as if she were touching herself. As a child she had been taught by her mother to always conduct herself as if someone were watching, to learn to behave like a "young lady under any circumstance."

The blue dress made her puzzled eyes look even bluer as with the arc of her smile she tried to bridge the chasm inside her, the way a rainbow makes a bridge between the rain and the sunlight. The dance was already in full swing. It seemed as if it were going to be a good farewell party.

A woman, looking very Jewish, and with a cross on a gold chain around her neck, told her partner, "Maybe you never were home to see the everyday beauty, so you can't leave when you were not there in the first place."

Somebody else said, "Only five minutes. Then we can talk in bed."

A fat man from the Sudeten asked her to dance. They were playing a slow waltz. She was pretty sure, when he asked her—in French spoken with a guttural German accent—"May I have the pleasure?" that he had just swallowed a last bit of smoked salmon. He smacked at her hand.

"My name is Kaiser, professor of drill, which means teacher of the strictest management, as measured only by military achievements. Former officers are perfect for it. Our enterprise includes over a hundred and fifty employees. Some people are touchy where this innocent and good world is concerned," he explained. Then he added, "It's a wonderful evening. It reminds me of the future just as much as of the past. Do you think the present is important at all?" Then, "Your arms are like the necks of white swans, Fräulein."

"Are you here with your wife?" Dita responded. He grinned. "Last week, at a graduation dance in my home town, I met a girl I used to go to school with and almost married. A beautiful love affair, as they say. But only in those days, I guess. She had the same blond hair, the same bittersweet smile and lovely blue eyes that you have."

"You don't dance badly either," she said.

"What do you think of America, young lady?"

"I think I'm immune."

Should she ask if he wore his old army decorations inside his vest? *Für treue Dienste in der SS,* for instance. He really did dance well. Feeling his strong hands and smelling his eau de cologne, she felt almost dizzy.

"If we learn how to lie well enough, we'll live to see better days," he said. "May I have the pleasure when they play a polka?"

She could imagine how a few years ago he would have been able to order her to take a hot bath and to remove her clothes, perhaps leaving her in her underwear.

The man said all of a sudden, "In the spring of 1945 the Russians occupied the castle of Bismarck von Osten in Pomerania. There wasn't a single German man there."

"All of them, even the old ones, had run away?"

"The castle was being looked after by Frau Hofeditz and her seventeen-year-old daughter, Gerda, who had been looking forward to the finest kind of a future, no matter how the war would turn out for the Germans," the man said almost reproachfully. She could imagine him striding through some prison camp, well fed and strong, complacent with his vision of how the world was going to look for the next thousand years, wearing a uniform tailored by some "inferior" Jew for the German superman, with his 9-mm pistol and his riding crop, the kind with a little lead bead at the end. Or a whip braided of curly black hair. He probably hadn't been as fat then, nor had he complained about losing his memory. "One cold February night a couple of Russian army trucks drove into the courtyard and raped Frau Hofeditz and her daughter and everything in reach that wore skirts. The name of the place was Plathe. Nobody could imagine how these two ladies must have looked when they were told that they had a disease as old as the history of rape. They were treated by a Jewish doctor, a certain Dr. Arndt, who had survived for six years in Germany living like a submarine."

Dita avoided answering.

"The younger woman told him about the terrible nights she'd spent in a cold sweat, full of panic every time they heard a truck engine," the man went on. "She described how her mother had tried to commit suicide. The doctor wanted to help them. But the old woman said, 'Don't try to save me. I don't want to live anymore.' Two weeks later she had shriveled up completely. She refused to eat and drink. She died of shame. They buried her in the castle graveyard."

Dita kept silent again. She lowered her chin and looked at him like a bull looking at a matador. Or like a dog about to bite.

Should he tell her that what was true last night wasn't necessarily so today? Or that—in their mutual interest—they mustn't allow themselves to depreciate what had happened yesterday and to divide it into good and bad, right and wrong? Because such measurements were obsolete, to say the least. Shouldn't he also tell her that, no matter how she chose to look at it, the thing that gave him greatest joy about what had happened was comparing it with what was still to come? And that, in comparison, what had happened would look like an innocent Sunday excursion?

"After a while the doctor noticed a change in Gerda's behavior. And when she'd talk about how the soldiers had raped her over and over, she'd laugh. Quietly at first, then out loud. For every soldier, she made a notch by the door. It turned out she'd infected seventy-five soldiers, so they shot her. In the courtyard before she was killed she said it was for her mother and that she didn't want to live anymore either."

"Ladies and gentlemen," announced the host, "it's ladies' choice." And he took his wife's hand. Everybody applauded.

Dita looked around for the twin brothers. They very seldom danced. They looked rather mild and content. When there were lulls in the dancing and conversation, they didn't go looking for anyone. For some reason, everything in her focused on them. She clung to her smile and her eyes glowed warmly again. She was glad when the dance ended. She walked out onto the balcony, moving across the dance floor as if it were ice. She could see her reflection in it, upside down.

She yearned for Slavic leisureliness, even though she never longed for German thoroughness. She asked herself what there was in her that was so deeply Jewish, even though she was blond and didn't pray?

Stars glittered in the sky. They were bright and clear, and the pines and firs whispered like invisible shadows. But the darkness outside was not complete. There was a full moon. She also saw the lovely Slavic forests and meadows, the gentle hills and the fragment of the Slavic soul that had entered into her and mingled with what was Jewish in her, and what was German too, because she had lived too long in Germany and occupied Poland during the war for that not to have left its traces. How much can we explain away? What do we believe in? What has man gone through, and how is it that by himself, from somewhere in the depths of his soul, he knows that he will still go through much more, whatever it might be?

An icy breeze blew down from the glacier. Yet in the air from the valley that touched her cheeks she could already smell the indefinable scent of the spring and the meadows. She felt a strange intense kind of weariness, as if she knew that something that had taken a long time was finally going to happen, but she didn't know what. The world rolled on through the darkness, and spring pressed through the air. But she didn't see it, any more than the stars did.

This was how spring came, year after year. People always wanted to experience something wonderful. Yet you've always got to think about needing money and other people. It certainly would be nice to have lots of friends and lots of money. No more tedious appeals, no more fifty-franc notes from D. E. She would have a hundred, a thousand times more! Maybe she'd steal it, the way Neugeborn wanted to do last year. Sure, when one is rich there are always friends, but when one is poor then comes the loneliness. In the room behind her they were playing some endless English waltz.

She stretched her arms out into the darkness. Behind her she felt warmth on her back. And with her forehead she touched the night and the cold. She was waiting for the Wehrli twins, but she didn't even need to turn around. She could feel the soft music and the cold from the glacier, and she realized that she might have to stand out here for hours and finally end up on the shelf after all.

4

"Why did you go away?" one of them said. "Aren't you cold out here?"

"Don't you think you're overdoing it?" the second brother asked.

"There was a door here," she answered.

In her voice something had replaced her old secret feeling of superiority.

"A lioness doesn't feed herself on little herbs," she said.

They took her back inside and showed her the house. She brought some of the early spring night with her. She looked at the paintings.

"That's Salvador Dali, father's pride," said the second brother. "That one is Hieronymus Bosch. Worth 400,000 marks."

"Do you know Kafka?" the first brother asked her. His voice was deeper.

"Like my own self," she said casually.

"There's never been anyone here from Prague before," the second boy said.

"Did you have any difficulties getting here?" asked the first.

"All I know is that in Basel two Italians almost got into a fist fight over who was going to carry my suitcases."

"What'll we drink to?" asked the second.

They sipped champagne.

"I met the brother of a friend of mine who died during the war here," Dita said. "And then I lost him again. He hadn't heard a word about his brother. He was a nice person. A painter, with quite a reputation by now. He carries his whole past around with him. He has a white house in a part of the country that looks like Bohemia. He spends most of his time working in the garden. He's got a studio and a record player and records that he plays over and over because otherwise, he says, he can't work. He keeps talking all the time about the Czech landscape. He claims that's what he paints. But you wouldn't recognize it; it's all abstract. He has two cars, three really, because he just bought another for his nineteen-year-old son. He doesn't budge from his house and his flowers except sometimes in the winter. He's got another house in town. His wife is Swiss. He's unhappy about the way things have developed since the war. She keeps worrying about what will become of their children, because they no longer have grandparents on his side. Nothing bad has ever happened to her all her life. When I left them, I felt for the first time that I really envied somebody. Not because of the white house or the cars or the garden or because he can do what he wants to do. But because they can afford to think about the past and worry about the future."

Then she said, "They are going to America. People always try to solve their problems by going from one place to the other as if the solution were in a change of place."

"Don't you like it here?" the first brother asked.

"That's not quite the right word for it," she responded. "I guess I liked it back home. I didn't want to leave like the others did. To betray something I'd be sorry for later. But when you add it all up, the fact is here I am and it is rather pleasant."

5

The brothers' room was arranged as a combination library and bedroom. A fire was burning in the fireplace. There was a big tile stove and rugs covered the floor, including a few sheepskins and a large lion's skin. The antique walnut furniture seemed well preserved and well oiled. The arms of the old chairs, obviously the work of some skilled cabinetmaker, were carved in the shape of crocodile jaws. You could even stick your fingers inside. Magnolias grew in knee-high flowerpots. There were a few still lifes on the wall and another painting of a path, this one leading along a lake with a coppery green surface.

"You've got a nice place here," she murmured.

"Please make yourself at home."

"You're sure you don't feel cold?"

"Oh no, on the contrary, it's very pleasant here."

"Can we get you anything?"

"No, thank you," she said, and she was thinking how everybody calls home any place where there's a roof over his head. It would be nice if every time you were under a roof you really did feel at home.

Why doesn't time evaporate this sentimental fog? Why does it only remind us of where we no longer are and make it harder to become part of the present?

The thought of money had already left her, and along with it went any resistance she might have felt when she entered the room. There was no longer any reason to tease them or to make fun of their nice clothes and their slightly pompous air as she'd wanted to do at first. Yet she hadn't lost the deeper idea of money as the basis of everything she needed and wanted—or that if she ever did take it from anyone (she clung to this idea like Neugeborn), she would find some way of giving it back later. She looked at the clock. It made a nice sound.

"I don't like it when nobody says anything," she said.

"Don't just leave it up to us," the first said.

"What'll we drink?" asked the second.

"You have a lovely bracelet," said the first one.

She smiled and her white teeth gleamed. The crackling fire was reflected brightly in her eyes and in her flushed cheeks. She could see herself in the mirror, and after a while, by the way the two brothers were looking at her, she knew how she must look. Whores can at least be pretty, she thought.

The night shone through the room. The stars had grown brighter than at the beginning of the party. The air was still, but the glass kept out the calm dark whispering sounds of the mountains and the trees, of the snow-covered alpine cliffs and the peaks that rose close to the sky.

"How do you feel?" the first brother asked.

"Like I'm sitting next to a nice fire," she replied.

"Are you homesick?"

"My eyes are full of light," she said, gazing into the fire. She lifted the corners of her mouth as if she were smiling to herself. With the fingers of her free hand she turned the bracelet around several times. She looked at her wrist with its circle of gold. The second brother uncorked a new bottle. She turned, wide-eyed, and looked at them. "This game used to be played for stakes, but I don't need that," she said. "I can't imagine how all this happened. I never expected anything like it. I feel a little bit drunk."

The first brother put a record on the big record player. They waited a moment for the first tune.

" 'Ti-pi-tin,' " she remarked in her singsong voice, not knowing exactly why she said it. " 'One night when the moon was so mellow, Rosita met young Manuelo.' " She smiled.

"Does it remind you of something?" asked the first brother as he poured the wine.

"Let's drink up," suggested the second brother.

"How fast?" she asked.

"Not how much?" the first brother wanted to know.

It was a German champagne, in elegant light green bottles with white labels, and black letters. The windows were large, and they could see a wide fragment of the night sky. They exchanged smiles and toasts across the rims of their glasses. Her face was turned toward the dark, so they didn't see her blushing.

"You've probably lived through a lot more than we have," said the first brother.

"I just left that category." She smiled. She could recall an occasion when she had said exactly the same thing to Mr. Gotlob in Prague.

"Did you know so many people were coming?" she asked.

"We're safely alone here," the second brother replied.

"Doesn't anybody ever come upstairs?"

"You don't need to be scared," the first reassured her.

"Probably on an evening like this our grandmothers would have been perfectly happy to have listened to some love poems and a little music on the lute, and that would have been that."

She curled up the corners of her lips in an adult smile. "Sometimes I think if I'd been born a few years earlier I'd probably be collecting stamps," she said. "The essential thing is to make a decision, and yet everything's relative. Why does the road back always seem shorter than the road going?"

To start with, they danced. She left her purse with the letters under an armchair. She slipped across the soft carpet, and the words they murmured meant very little compared to the triple strength that enveloped them. The windows were bright from the outside, but from the inside they were dark mirrors that reflected the quiet intensity of the brothers' eyes, the laughter of their lips, and the fact that she had attracted them and made them invite her upstairs. The windows were like a visible and transparent borderline between the darkness of the night outside and the light within; they reflected a division in herself, a grief for what was over, and a fear of what was now to begin. They savored the contrast between the noise of the crowd downstairs and the calm, strange dance they were doing up here.

The first brother put "Ti-pi-tin" back on the phonograph and stared at her, not saying a word. She pulled away from the second brother and put her ear against the door.

"You smell of cleanliness," he said at first. "You're wonderfully clean."

"What would you say if I weren't?" She smiled.

"Are you alone?" the first brother asked.

"Alone?"

"Aren't you the one they say saved some children during the war?" the second brother asked.

She felt again that strange kind of tension she had felt when she was with D. E. at the Hotel Astoria/Novak, formerly Yellow Stone Inn. Then too she had known exactly why she'd come, what she wanted to do and why, and what a surprise it would be. It was like a circle, always closed.

With a smile on her lips, she wondered, Who can feel more alone than children without parents, than parents without children, husbands without wives, and wives without husbands? She continued to smile. She would never be able to say it to anyone.

The record was almost half over, and the second brother took her hand in his and drew her to the other side of the room. He looked into her eyes without saying a word, as if he were asking her to tell him something about herself—or, quite the contrary, to keep quiet. Perhaps he was trying to decide what it was about her that irritated him.

She closed her eyes in expectation. It was like crossing the threshold of a room she had never entered before. She didn't know for sure what would happen. She'd always wanted something that both the brothers had without even trying very hard.

A person needs somebody to love her like a little child. Because she's going from one country to another? For some other reason? No matter how it is, it's very difficult to get along without this love.

Again she had the feeling she was on a train that was rushing on regardless of any timetable and the only way she could get off would be to jump. The train was going at such a speed that nobody could slow it down or stop it. It made her dizzy.

As they danced, she tried to decide which brother was which. She looked the first one in the eyes as intently as he looked at her. He kissed her shoulders and neck and temples and she didn't stop him, just as later she didn't stop either of them in any way. At first, when she noticed that his voice was deeper, she felt she had discovered something.

"You don't have to apologize," she whispered. "I won't either."

Both brothers had the same eyes—large, greenish-brown, and relaxed, without any mud-colored rings underneath like fat Munk's. These eyes were deep-set, as if they came from Southern stock. The dance music was beautiful, not too fast or too loud, the kind of music she'd always loved, the kind that had always made her feel better.

"Well," she whispered. "I hope it's O.K. Everybody takes care of himself now." And to herself she added what it was she'd just left.

She had been a little afraid at first. What if their father should suddenly decide to come into this room? But the feeling passed. She didn't know their first names, and she was far from sure they knew her last name.

She went on with her seduction as they danced. She watched the brothers through her dark lashes, dancing with them in turn, her breasts pressed tightly to their chests. Among the records they played were "Bei Mir Bist Du Schön," "Mama Inez," and "Siboney." She guessed they must have been here almost an hour by now. The last tune was as sweet as it had been for her in her best days, wherever they had been.

"I don't even know you yet," she whispered. "But, then, talking only spoils things." She paused. "Life isn't what we want but what we have. It's true you know, but sometimes it hurts to admit it, and it costs us a good many tears before we can bear to face it. Just forget what I said about stamp collecting." All urgency was gone from her voice. The brothers locked the door and then put out the light.

As she danced, Dita studied their teeth, the same ivory color as hers. She studied their mouths before, abruptly and gravely, she touched their lips, then their necks, while she pressed herself closer, first to one, then to the other. The light was dim and indistinct, merging with the night and the hills and the pine forest. Everything seemed to be loosening and uncoiling and breathing freely inside her; it became increasingly pleasant, pure, and beautiful, even when she felt their fingers touching her naked flesh. She kissed their throats, pressing closer and closer to them, caressing their bodies with her palms while their hands moved all over her body. She found herself kissing them on the mouth, her lips turning to theirs and opening of their own accord. It was like an exciting game of opposites. Something was happening that none of them had ever experienced. The clock chimed. Its pendulum glowed in the dark. They could hear cars driving away, and voices and other noises from downstairs. A charged silence filled the room. She no longer wore her blue taffeta dress. She was dancing finally in the darkness with almost nothing on at all, as tall as they were, white and supple. They danced in the dark, their only lamp mounted on a bamboo ship, curved like a drawn bow, glowing from the reflection of the snow outside. Nothing had been spoken for some time. None of them felt outraged by anything. She turned her face away.

She stretched out on one of the fur rugs. She rolled over to her side on the lion skin and drew her legs up. She kept wishing the next few moments would pass quickly. The clock chimed again, three quarters of an hour. Everything seemed to close in on her, a combination of heat and silence. The next time it struck, it was twelve o'clock.

"No more," she heard herself saying.

"Why not?" the first brother asked.

"That's enough," she said defensively, her own voice sounding alien to her. She smoothed her hair and ran her hands down over her flanks, and leaning against the wall, just as she was, she said quietly, "The last few minutes of March the twenty-second. Now I'm nineteen years old." Only nineteen, or ten times as much?

The fire flickered on the hearth, like a cave dug into a cliff. Its sides were plastered with rough mortar.

"I guess I'm not the most appreciative soul in the world," she said. It grew into a sort of upside-down apology, at first only an echo, quiet, then growing stronger.

The record changer stopped. She looked through the glass

at the trees and the snow. But most of all she saw the door. She realized that the time she had pleaded for her mother in the fall of 1944 she'd really been pleading to go with her.

"I hope you won't think too harshly of me," she said. "And even if you do, life's harder for a weak person." She turned the bracelet on her wrist.

I'm a whore, she said to herself. No doubt about it. As Andy said, every whore was once a virgin. Only whores behave like this, just to buy a little warmth and company and some prospects for tomorrow, changing the rules after the game has started. And should she go on doing this for another fifty years, day after day? And what if she did it in the respectable way, instead, as someone's wife—just for a slice of daily bread, a piece of legal paper, and the privileges of a married woman—would there then be the sort of outcry in the night so familiar to Tonitchka Blauova? Would anyone like to hear something she'd never told anyone before? She felt again like someone who suddenly stops and has the feeling that he's been asleep for a long time and has just awakened. Again she was on that train that went on and on, and she couldn't get off. She couldn't stop it. Is it only because I have been where I have been, or would it be the same in any case? She excused and accused herself at the same time. It was as if there were an invisible glass wall between them. What is true needn't look probable.

On her oval face, the whole time, was her mild adult smile.

6

"Are you still here?" the first brother asked out of the darkness.

"It's not your fault," she said.

"Should I switch on the light?" he asked.

"For a proud person, every dream dies twice," Dita said, smiling.

"Sure, we're all from far away." The second brother chuckled. "Just to make sure, I'll put out another bottle of wine to chill."

In her mind she was talking to Fitzi Neugeborn. That's the

difference between you and me, Fitzi, she said. It's the difference between Neugeborn the dreamer and Dita the realist. You are happy enough just imagining what nice children we could have, while I am imagining the disaster just around the corner even in moments of happiness.

The first brother stood up. He took down the painting of the lakeside path. "It's for you," he said.

"I don't want any more gifts," she said. And she thought about what it was that made her do things, and she thought about her mother.

"You should," the first brother said.

The worst of it is, I'm not behaving like a good whore or even a bad one, she thought.

"I'm beginning to think the world's not the best place for me," she said. There was that unreal smile on her lips.

"In Birkenau, in 1944, before a selection, a girl told me not to give your whole soul to anything or anybody," she remarked. "Otherwise it's too awful, she said, when you lose it. It can be a person, a country, a relationship. Expectations or wishes. It breaks you up into so many pieces that you can't get back together again."

She was wondering about her mother, and how her father had behaved during those last moments, or next to last. It seemed almost indecent to think about it. Not even the most candid witness will ever tell absolutely all there is to tell.

"Shame probably isn't the best judge," she said after a while.

She thought about the girls who had suddenly started laughing for no reason at all. "Everything's lovely," she said slowly. "Everything's all right." Suddenly she laughed. It struck her as funny. She looked through the window at the sky.

"You should give it a little rest now," said the first one again. "What are you going to do?"

"Next time I'll be better prepared," she answered with a smile.

"You should come again," the second brother said. It was as if he had asked in his mind, "And that's all?"

"It's not just a game for me," Dita answered. The heavy feeling in her stomach disturbed her. "Sometimes it is hard for me to be the carefree girl you imagine." She smiled hazily as if she were glowing inside, but it showed through only in fractured beams of light. They exchanged good nights and smiles. The words were no longer important. The second brother switched on the lights in the hall and in front of the villa. She allowed both of them to kiss her on the lips once more. She asked them not to see her out.

The sidewalk was empty. She could hardly believe that she had just turned nineteen. Nineteen years. Two evanescent, almost unreal resignations of her body.

7

It was a frosty dawn. The stars had melted away; they were no longer like bright clusters of grapes. She remembered vaguely that she should have said thank you. I'm a little bit drunk, but not much, she said to herself.

The snow had a hard crust. Its surface was firm and very white and it gleamed as if it had been sprinkled with stardust. A rooster shattered what was left of the night with his welcome to the morning. His crow echoed from the mountainsides. Wind blew through the open lungs of the ravine.

A hill of ice and snow reared up in front of her. She was not at all tired. The glacier looked quite accessible, like some familiar place she'd visited many times before. She stopped for a few moments, out of breath. The overhanging walls of snow were solid and almost comforting. The crowns of the pine trees waved gently back and forth. There were warning signs and safety chains. It was ridiculous to go up there in the shoes she was wearing. Far away she could see stretches of mountain forests, pine and fir trees, and inaccessible gorges where no one had ever been. The snow was firm and crisp, and she found that she could walk on it without difficulty.

When the first edge of the sun became as bright as the stars had been in the middle of the night, she had climbed to the very spot she'd so often dreamed of. She decided to wait there for the new day. The mirror of ice reflected the big round image of the morning sun as it dawned full and red.

Far below, life began, as always, with the sun. Everything was virgin pure and white. Entranced, she gazed down at the countryside beneath her. It lay at her feet untouched, the valley with its back to the mountains and its face open to the sun, from one end of the horizon to the other, the great burden and treasure of the world. Why was man born? Why had she been born? And why as the creature she was? Could a permanent invitation be found anywhere, any sense of security to rid her of her persistent fear of tomorrow? And was it possible to get anything without having to humiliate yourself in the process?

She breathed in the icy morning air. She felt a pressure in her stomach. She squinted. She could hear the wind. She could smell the sweet scent of pine resin, and she could still taste last night's wine. She smoothed her hair. She was getting hungry. But she didn't want to hurry.

What was she supposed to lean on in her thoughts? How had she lived up to now? How had she prepared herself, during all those greater and lesser defeats that had befallen her, for what was still to come?

It was almost like the joke D. E. used to tell in Prague, about how 90 percent of the people thought we had an easy life, without the necessity of effort. And the other 10 percent? "They don't matter—they're *us*."

Where can I possibly go, limping along as if I had one leg instead of two, when I need to run; one arm instead of two, when I need to grasp things firmly in my hands; and one eye instead of two, when I need to see things as they are? What can I do to be happy? She could hear the echo. Do whatever you want, since there's nowhere to go.

She had made a long journey from the chimneys in Poland—from fire, smoke, and ashes, and from the longing in Prague—to this morning, to this place and this moment; and she knew it.

She looked down. Nothing was melting up above the village. She kept hearing all the songs she had ever liked. Why do some people know how to live and others keep making one mistake after another? Why is one person tough and purposeful while another blindly believes he can wear his heart on his sleeve? Why do some people find what they're looking for and others keep blundering around in the clouds, unfaithful to today's dreams, but perhaps faithful and dependable, as she was, somewhere inside?

She felt the sun and at the same time the fresh wind. The countryside was beautiful, though cold. Everything seemed translucent as never before.

Why had she been given a soul that could be wounded by things others managed to ignore? Why could she bear the loss of her parents, yet not be able to sit on the side of the road like a beggar?

She turned up her coat collar. Could she still accept the boat ticket to El Salvador? Do I still have a chance to cash in my chips and just go? To dandle redheaded kiddies on my knee while yearning for some phantom that probably doesn't even exist? What would I have over there? An emigrant, a foreigner who has nothing in common with anybody except the black servant girls who will bring me my breakfast in bed? There will be a war and my husband, my son, will have to go. Why? For El Salvador? For America? For the German side? What was the use of going there? What was the use of going on?

She drew in great drafts of cold and fragrant air, and suddenly she felt strong.

All that remained in her memory was this last night, no longer in its particular warmth, in its pleasant and affectionate details, but rather as a kind of summing-up of all her nineteen years. Why had she been born? What would it be like if she presented herself at the twins' house tonight, or tomorrow night? Probably the same as if she accepted that ticket to El Salvador.

She tossed her hair out of her eyes and laughed to herself. Things had never turned out the way she wanted them to, and she never wanted things the way they were. Life is not what we want but what we have. She was amazed at how simple the answer was when it finally occurred to her.

Suddenly she could feel it all. The hurt pride and vanity, the fear of the future, and the disappointment proportionate to all she had expected. Helplessness, fear, and loneliness—fragments of feelings that grew into a deep pain.

The sun was now rising over the mountains and valleys; and as the night retreated step by step and second by second, morning was born. Her eyes were tired and defiant. They didn't look like those eyes that register only the simple fear of a world that had so far been so very kind. She felt ready to embrace the world, to put it all on and wear it like a veil.

The snow, the trees, and the mountains were filled with a morning light that grew clearer and clearer. She tried to find a connection in her mind between all the things that kept coming back to her even as she thought they were disappearing—as if she weren't two jumps ahead. It was like the wall between the living and those who are dead or still unborn, or the wall between fear and freedom, between helplessness and hope. She looked down at the earth that stretched out before her, clean and pure. She looked up at the sky, which rose out of infinity and then lost itself in the distance. Who knew when the snow would start to melt? She drew up her collar. Nobody had any respect for weaklings.

She remembered how they'd sung in camp one time. The song was as beautiful as everything that has to do with being free, with a clear conscience, with each person having a fair share, with trust in the fate of each one who survives at an acceptable price—that it's possible to lose your innocence, but you mustn't lose dignity or that portion of self-confidence that keeps your head above water.

But as she heard the echoes of that song in her mind, she realized how irrevocably the melody was disappearing, the lyrics and the mood, and with them the song's meaning and its promise. She felt as if she were trying to catch all of that—reaching for it with hands outstretched, as a person might reach out to touch the future. In that moment she understood it all so clearly that it chilled her. The feeling was so real that as she looked down she saw her own hands in front of her, reaching out as if to protect her from whatever she might run into. She felt a throbbing pain between her thighs.

Very slowly she went closer to the edge, nearer to the sun. Now the new day was here, like a gift just for her, waiting, a beautiful dawn, as bright as she had ever seen before.

A moment later, when there was no more edge and she slipped and fell, her body struck against the rocks and ice. As she tried to catch herself, something suddenly hit her head and dazed her. It felt as if she were pulling down with her all the snow and the rocks that were in her way.

The snow she fell through made a whistling sound like the wind or like an avalanche, and as she began to fall, in the echo of the rocks she heard long sentences she would never be able to pronounce. For a split second she saw the blue waters of a land she'd never seen before. And then there were only those three things on her mind.

She couldn't think anymore about how many rocks she'd drag down with her before she reached the bottom. She knew that none of them would stop her, that she'd go on pushing them in front of her, faster and faster. At first she felt it all in darkness, then washed with a strong light, and finally dark again. She no longer knew where up was or where down was either.

There was no up-and-down anymore. Everything finally melted away, including her fear that she might cause difficulties for somebody, and including the shock of the impact on the delicate skin that was the color of an unripe peach.

8

Later, on the evening of that same March day, the mailman delivered a letter addressed to Dita Saxova. It was from Erich Munk in Prague.

"I wish you all possible luck, Dita," he wrote at the end. "May your life prove to be both what you want and what you have, whether you decide to reply to me or not, or whatever you may choose to do in the future. My dear Dita Saxova, every slice of bread we eat has two sides to it. I kiss you."

Since the addressee was no longer there, the letter was returned.